The Tortois

Fanny Frewen was born in 1924. At seventeen she ran away from home to become a Gunner on an Anti-Aircraft Site. After the war she went to Drama School and then worked on *Vanity Fair* and *Harper's Bazaar* before making her career in advertising where she wrote, among others, the first eighteen Oxo commercials. She now lives in Kent with her husband, Stephen, and writes full time.

To Stephen Frewen
who has endured many years of marriage to the author
with kindness and with love

THE TORTOISE SHELL

Fanny Frewen

ARROW

I

Mrs Boxendale did not bear widowhood with fortitude. No fortitude was needed. It was the happiest state of her life, one of the great benefits of old age.

For Mrs Boxendale, being old had, in any case, a lot more going for it than had being young. At ninety-five one creaked a bit, of course, and sometimes a laugh or a cough took one's bladder by surprise. Pity one couldn't be a brisk eighty again. Mrs Boxendale's eightieth birthday had heralded the first year of her widowhood. She was lucky, in more ways than one, to be a widow.

Although it was hardly the fault of the women made surplus by the First World War, unmarried females knew themselves to be the objects of ridicule and condescension, just as they had always been. A spinster pushing thirty married what she could get. And what Cecilia Gifford got was Reginald Boxendale.

Reginald Boxendale begat upon her two children, Nigel and Betty. The begetting was not too disagreeable. Not pleasant, certainly not enjoyable, simply what came with achieving the status of being a married woman. Even now, all these years later, she still wore her wedding ring, loose on the nobbly old finger. That it had cost her fifty years of boredom and irritation made no difference. She had got her commission and this was its badge of rank.

Even without the war, Cecilia Gifford knew she was not endowed with the qualities that appealed to the young men of her generation. A girl five foot eleven inches tall could hardly be kittenish. She bicycled faster than the boys and she beat them at tennis as well. She couldn't resist the joy of speeding along on her bike and was too honest to muff her shots. Her mother, a rosebud, despaired of her ill-luck in producing a daughter who took after her tall, hawk-nosed husband instead of her dainty self. Mr Gifford made up for his over-lively contribution to this disaster by addressing Cecilia as Telegraph Pole and advising her to run her nose against the door a few times if she ever hoped to get a husband. That she was to become a handsome, upright old lady was not much good to a young girl who towered over all women and quite a few men, who would have been hit in the eye by Cecilia's nose in the unlikely event of their trying to kiss her.

Old Mrs Boxendale was very fond of her house in Tiddingfold High Street. It had a small front garden, hardly a garden at all, just a mahonia and a rose behind white palings and a short path to the front door. Its glory was its back garden, the largest behind any house in the High Street.

She would never have been able to persuade Reginald to buy it if Nigel hadn't been killed in 1942. Had Nigel lived, nothing would have persuaded Reginald Boxendale to give up the Victorian mock-Tudor mock-manor that was to have been his son's inheritance. He was fonder of his daughter than of his son but that was neither here nor there; one did not leave one's property to daughters. So if Cecilia wanted this inconvenient, poky, un-modernised cottage he could afford to let her have it. In fact, he could afford it very well indeed, since his grief at the loss of his heir was not so overwhelming as to destroy his satisfaction at coming out of the exchange with an extremely large fistful of change.

Nigel was dead and Betty had left home to teach primary school and share flats with other teachers who had nicknames; so Reginald could see no need, with just the two of them left, to dip into his sturdy bank account for such fripperies as central heating, a modern cooker to replace the ancient kitchen range, a washing machine or domestic help. He did, however, see every need for breakfast, morning coffee, luncheon, tea and dinner with pre-war standards as to napery and silver. Any attempt to present him with a shop-bought cake or a freezer dinner brought on a grim, silent furore.

If Cecilia complained of being cold, he told her to take some exercise. She'd been an athletic girl, hadn't she? But that was the trouble with women, they gave up and got lazy, whereas he marched the golf course with his bag of golf clubs on his shoulder. No caddies or trolleys for him! Reginald knew the meaning of self-discipline as no one else, in his opinion, did. He died proving it. He caught cold, lingering at the eighteenth hole to avoid buying a round of drinks in the clubhouse and expired a few days later. Cecilia, anointing her chilbains, suddenly became not only a widow but also a well-off widow.

The first thing Mrs Boxendale did after probate was to order a dozen bottles of good sherry and instal central heating. The old kitchen range made a sturdy base upon which to place a Baby Belling. She would have had a microwave instead, if she had ever heard of such a thing, for she was done with cooking for ever. She thrived on celery, tomatoes, cream cheese on crackers and, if she wanted something hot, fish fingers: quite delicious once she had overcome her confusion about fish having fingers.

One of her greatest new pleasures was Lucy dropping in. Lucy was, quite simply, Mrs Boxendale's best friend. In fairness, you could never say that Reginald didn't like her. Quite the contrary, he idolised her, for Lucy was Lady Lucy Dormer, wife of Mr Peter Dormer, a Lady in her own right, daughter of an Earl. But the very thought of Cecilia receiving Lucy in her winceyette nightgown or her gardening trousers would probably have preceded the pneumonia that had carried him off by a heart attack. In Reginald's lifetime, Lady Lucy Dormer was only let into the house for a dinner party with polished candlesticks.

On a beautiful morning in spring, Mrs Boxendale stood up in her garden with mud all over her trousers. She had been kneeling to pull a few weeds out and praise the daffodils. A blackbird was making its nest in the cherry tree. It was time for sherry and a salty biscuit, a treat she enjoyed alone and even more when, as often happened, Lucy came in to share it.

'Chip-chip-chip.' Something must be agitating the blackbird. Probably a cat. The high street was full of fashionable cats these days: Siamese, Burmese, Lord knew what; with names like

3

Ho-Chi-Min and Clarence. But they caught birds as relentlessly as the kitties of yore.

There was no cat in the garden but someone was coming through the narrow passageway beside the house. Lucy never came that way. Lucy could have come in any way she chose, but she always knocked at the front door. 'Halloo-oh,' called a voice that spelt doom to a pleasant morning. Mrs Phillips, the doctor's wife. Mrs Boxendale sat down on the grass and pretended to be weeding.

'Yoo-hoo. Busy in your garden, I see.' Mrs Boxendale made no reply. 'Good for you. But that wet grass! Not good for the old rheumatism.'

'I do not have rheumatism. Who are you?' She was damned if she'd let the woman into the house and be told again that salted biscuits weren't good for the old blood pressure. Funny how doctors always married nurses who subsequently out-doctored them. If she says Ups-a-daisy, I may kill her.

'Ups-a-daisy.' Mrs Phillips put a hand under Mrs Boxendale's arm and almost tipped her over on to her face. In spite of any effort she could make, Mrs Boxendale found herself dragged up on to her feet and hauled indoors. 'Mustn't overdo it. I expect your dear husband used to do a lot in the garden.'

'Not as far as I can recollect,' replied Mrs Boxendale.

Mrs Phillips had not a sensitive ear. 'I'm sure you still miss him,' she droned on, 'poor you. I don't know what I'd do without my good man.'

'I'm sorry I can't ask you to stay, but I'm expecting a visitor,' said Mrs Boxendale firmly, well aware that Mrs Phillips was looking judgmentally at the sherry bottle on the coffee table. 'For lunch. And I have to make a soufflé.' Would the beastly woman fall for such a patent lie?

'Let me help you.'

'No, thank you.' Mrs Boxendale's look would have frozen out two double-glazing salesmen and a Jehovah's witness, but Mrs Phillips was not that easy to get rid of.

'I know what I came to tell you. We're putting on a pensioners' party at the W.I hall. I came specially to tell you first.'

'I'm afraid I can't help you. I don't bake at all these days, so I can't offer to make cakes for you.'

'No, no, I don't expect you to do anything like that. I'm inviting you as our guest. It's our annual do for the old folks who don't get out much, you know, so I naturally thought of you. We can pick you up; we'll be doing the rounds down at the council houses and we could collect you at the same time.'

Mrs Boxendale took in a deep breath. 'I smell petrol,' she said evenly. 'Maybe you forgot to switch off the engine of your motor-car. You had best go and drive it away.'

'Really,' said Mrs Phillips, sitting in her silent car, 'to think I only bother with her because I'm sorry for her and dear Lady Lucy is so fond of her.'

Mrs Boxendale took a sherry glass out of the corner cupboard, gave it a scornful glance and exchanged it for a wine glass, which she filled to the brim with Amontillado. She then went into the kitchen, took four salt biscuits and smothered them in full-fat cream cheese, to which she added a further sprinkle of salt. But before she settled down to her enjoyment, she paid one more short visit to her garden.

In her little potting-shed she found the chicken wire she sought. 'Thank goodness I'm tall,' she gasped as she reached up into the cherry tree. 'At least I don't have to fall off a stepladder and let that bloody woman get her hands on me.' She packed the wire efficiently round the nest, under the curious yellow eye of its blackbird tenant. 'There you are. It'll take some cat to get you now,' she told it, and marched indoors.

2

It was the nappies that brought them together. Lady Lucy married a poor man and Mrs Boxendale had married a mean one. Later, all that was changed. Peter Dormer achieved success and wealth and Mrs Boxendale achieved widowhood and wealth.

But at the time of her first baby's birth, Lucy had to find out more than she cared to know about nappies and Mrs Boxendale was glad to have long graduated.

Peter and Lady Lucy started their married life as the owners of a large house on the outskirts of Tiddingfold, and precious little else. The house was called Alexandra Lodge. The façade was stylish. The high-ceilinged drawing-room was furnished with chairs of elegant antiquity and great discomfort; Lucy's aristocratic mama had seized the opportunity to discard them as a wedding gift. With the money she saved, Lucy's mama bought herself the first comfortable chair she had ever sat upon. By the same token, Lucy's papa had presented them with a broken-legged escritoire and a map table in which the wood-worms held constant revel. He hadn't any money to save, being a popular Earl with the bookies, but he bought another horse just the same. Nevertheless Lady Lucy brought, as her portion, the very backdrop needed to advance the career of the young lawyer with whom she had fallen in love.

At little more than twenty years old and ignorant of domestic affairs, it was not until too late that Lucy came face to face with her share of the bargain. An underground servants' hall with no servants. One bathroom, in which you could have given a ball. Indeed it was better suited to holding a ball than having a bath, which involved either cold water or a dangerous encounter with a geyser that could have been conscripted as a secret weapon in any war.

The day Mrs Boxendale paid her call, Lucy was in tears over a burnt saucepan and a pile of stinking nappies. The baby, Jack, a nice chap who never complained unless there was something serious to complain about, was yelling his head off. He had a very sore bottom.

'I take it,' said Mrs Boxendale, trying not to sit too heavily on the chair in the cold drawing-room into which Lucy, drying her chapped hands, had shown her, 'that you would have a cook and a nanny if you could afford them?' She did not think of herself as being good with babies, but she jiggled the pram in which Jack was still crying. His ill-pinned nappy fell off. Straight away, feeling more comfortable, he beamed up at her. 'What a nice baby,' said Mrs Boxendale.

'He is. He's a darling baby. But I'm so bad at it. You see, I wanted to do it all myself.'

'Rats. No sane woman can possibly enjoy scouring saucepans or being a baby's lavatory attendant.' Mrs Boxendale glanced round the elegant drawing-room. She knew all about Peter Dormer. He already had Reginald's business. It wasn't difficult to see what Lucy was trying to achieve. No point in asking whether Papa could come up with the dibs to pay for a nanny and a cook. One knew that sort of Earl, filtered down through the mists of glorious wastefulness. 'Is your husband mean?' she asked abruptly.

'No. Not in the least.' This was true and something Lucy had to clarify to this piercing-eyed old lady she liked already. 'But . . .'

'But. His own mother never had a maid, never mind a nanny?'

Lucy smiled. 'That's exactly it. He's brilliant, you know. He got to Oxford on a scholarship. I don't want to let him down.'

'Right. Well, here's how we'll start.' Mrs Boxendale stood up. It was a relief for such a large woman to get out of that shaky chair without smashing it. She knew houses like this, and led the way, followed by Lucy, down into the dank-tiled depths below. 'Now,' she ordered, 'give me that saucepan. I am going to throw it into my own dustbin. Ditto these revolting nappies. They are beyond redemption.'

'But they're Harringtons' squares and terry-towelling,' wailed Lucy.

'I know. I've got dozens of the things, put away. How old is the baby?'

'Almost a year.'

'Right. Use mine up. Then chuck them away. I shall not have grandchildren.'

To Lucy, Mrs Boxendale became a dear friend. To Mrs Boxendale Lucy became dearer than her own daughter. Not that she had anything against Betty, but Betty didn't need her.

Betty, who cut her hair with the kitchen scissors only when it got in the way, started in on the love of her life, dog-breeding, even before she reached retirement from school. It was fair to say she did well with primary school children, treating, as she did, the little Traceys and Jasons with the same thumping demeanour as she gave the four-legged Taras and Princes. On the rare occasions that Betty telephoned her, Mrs Boxendale always ended up ringing off, confused as to which were children and which were dogs.

Betty now shared a bungalow with someone called Bobby. As far as Mrs Boxendale could make out, Bobby was a Miss Barbara Jenkins, and not a dog.

Little Jack became very fond indeed of Mrs Boxendale. 'You may call me Cecilia,' said Mrs Boxendale, when Jack was six. 'No,' said Jack firmly. 'You are Mrs Bockindale and I love you.'

Mrs Boxendale liked Jack. Not as a replacement for Nigel, not as the grandson she had never had, but as a friend. For one thing, he showed every sign of growing tall. How different her life might have been if it hadn't been for the rotten quirk of being, herself, taller than most of the men of her day. And she loved his energy. For all that he was shooting up fast, he was co-ordinated. It was she who taught him how to ride a bicycle and he who admired her own ability still to out-race him.

She didn't so much like little Penelope, who made her appearance five years after Jack. Looking into the newly-filled cradle, Mrs Boxendale recognised a Missy little girl. Penelope took her back to those long-ago days, way back before the war . . . The First World War, she had to remind herself, not the Second, which had done in Nigel . . . and remembered. Before she was two years old, Penelope had the power to revert Mrs Boxendale to the awkward, lanky, long-nosed girl who had eventually been married by Reginald Boxendale before it was too late. Penelope was a rosebud.

And now, Penelope was engaged to be married. To a young man called Brian Transom. Mrs Boxendale was happy for her.

But what was much more interesting was that Jack had brought home, to meet his mother and father, a young woman called Henny Brack.

It was Peter Dormer's greatest pride to have sent his boy to Eton. As it turned out, Jack was no great academic. But, by the time he was fifteen he was already pushing towards six feet in height. And, although not a pick of fat was on him, he was sturdy enough to do what he was best at, which was to play games. He had no enormous opinion of himself. Indeed, he could hardly believe the captainships – of football and of cricket – that came his way. He took an 'Oh well, if you say so' view of being captain. It was just a means of going on playing and he hardly noticed the smaller boys who followed him adoringly. He only observed that some were more promising than others and ought to be encouraged. He was rather pleased when they did as he instructed them. It made for a better game and it was nice, in Jack's view, that they just did as he advised without making a fuss.

His father was less than enchanted with his academic reports; he had hoped the boy would become a barrister, an opportunity that he had never had. He made the best he could out of casual references to 'my son, captaining the Eton and Harrow this year', but secretly fretted over enormous fees and no signs of any promise of success in the world he understood, the world which had been such a struggle for him to get into.

As time went by, and Peter Dormer's practice flourished, Alexandra Lodge had become a much more comfortable home. Penelope had her own pony. She didn't ride well, but she turned out smartly and expensively at pony-club gymkhanas.

The way she kicked the pony was not attractive, but she hauled it over the jumps and smiled charmingly every time she received a cup or a red, green, blue or yellow rosette to pin on to the bridle.

Jack was not horsy. He wasn't even very fond of dogs. His favourite creature was a tortoise, which he bought with his own money. 'What can you see in the stupid thing?' Penelope asked scornfully, carrying her saddle.

'Mind your own business,' said Jack. He was not often sharp with Penelope. 'What do you see in your pony?'

'He loves me,' said Penelope. This was not true. The pony loved nobody. Penelope looked at the tortoise, who was eating a strawberry as Jack stroked his head. 'Eugh. It's a reptile.'

'I've named him Heraclitus,' said Jack. The name of his tortoise was the only thing he brought away from the Classical aspect of his education.

It was as much a surprise to Cecilia Boxendale as it was to Lucy Dormer when Jack went into the advertising business. Cecilia had had, subconsciously, dreams for Jack. He represented, growing tall and athletic, everything in a man she had been deprived of in her gawky, pre-1914 girlhood. She followed his athletic prowess at Eton, and imagined the Blue he would achieve at Oxford. She thought perhaps he would become an explorer, and play county cricket on his returns home.

Lucy Dormer was also taken aback at the news. She would be the first to admit that she didn't know a thing about advertising. But, at the same time, she thought of it as dangerously Londony. She knew perfectly well that she had no business to think of her tall, already shaving son as a little boy, sensitive to the requirements of his tortoise. Even so, even so. They made these television commercials and you could see that they flew all over the world just to advertise a chocolate bar. How would her Jack contend with those high-breasted models who didn't look kind at all?

It was the first open rift between Jack and his father. Peter Dormer, so proud of having got his boy to Eton, was already debating which Oxford college would crown his efforts. He felt he was generous in accepting Jack's lack of academic success but simply could not believe that an old Etonian could fail to get into Oxford. Worse was to follow. Prepared as he was to pay to get Jack into one of those colleges where charm and cricket would do, he was shattered when Jack made his ungrateful announcement.

'No. Thank you. I'm not going to university. I know you would have liked me to go to Balliol, as you did.'

'I hadn't,' said Peter, so angry that he spoke calmly, 'thought of Balliol. You haven't the brains.'

'There you are,' said Jack. 'You see what I mean? Why waste your money on getting me to Oxford, where I don't want to go and where I'd be lucky to get a pass degree if anything at all, when I have other plans?'

'And what are these plans?'

Jack hated to see his father striving to be patient in the face of infuriated disappointment. He hurried on. 'It's simple. I'm not that brilliant. Honestly, sir, I'd do much better just working. There was a boy in the cricket team when I was captain and his father's got an advertising agency. He's offered me a job. I want to take it.' Jack watched his father closely and added, 'And I'm going to take it.'

Lucy, much as she loved Peter, had never realised the triumph of his achievement. She just loved him. Her own inheritance was lost on her; she only knew she had a rather potty mama and a papa who gambled.

Peter was at Oxford when she met him. It was the way of things. Her brother was at Oxford. She herself had no education. Her brother had been to Eton and then on to Oxford, so it was natural he should take her to a May Ball. There, she met Peter. His mother and father lived in Slough. When Peter took her to their home she thought it was rather nice, a lot warmer than the castle in Ireland or the Place in Leicestershire. She married him.

Peter Dormer's father was a solicitor's clerk. His mother was a wife. They were modest people who had given birth to a clever, attractive, randy son. Even at grammar school, into which he had gained easy entry, Peter was a star. He knocked off his first girl at fifteen. Oxford held no terrors for him. His loving mother over-equipped him with a heavy, clerical grey suit that didn't quite fit. Quite ruthlessly, he hung it in the back of the cupboard in his rooms and went about in jeans and beery sweaters in instinctive imitation of inherited-wealth undergraduates.

He was in his third year when Lucy came his way. He married her because he loved her. Whether he would have fallen in the marrying kind of love if she had been the daughter of a Co-Op manager instead of an Earl was not put to the test.

Peter Dormer found it irritating that Penelope seemed to have inherited his firmness of purpose and Jack, as he chose to believe, only his mother's gentle, vague nature. What he wouldn't admit was that the prime cause of his uneasiness with his son was Jack's five-inch advantage in height. To have a wife who was the daughter of an Earl was a triumph. To produce a son who had tiresomely inherited his aristocratic grandfather's build, together with a cheerful disregard of study, was another.

But Peter Dormer had, above all, a clear way of looking at things. He privately thought of advertising as a rather silly business. But at least it was better to have a son in advertising than a son with a ponytail and cock-eyed ideas about saving whales or some such.

It was perfectly obvious that Jack was never going to follow him into the now flourishing country-town firm of Dormer and Gill, solicitors to the old money and the new. Penelope had the astuteness, but her interests did not lie that way. Penelope had no intention of becoming the first female lawyer in the county. Thank heavens. Peter Dormer had never admitted a woman to his practice.

Jack's burgeoning career in advertising served to conform his father's opinion of the trade. The salary his son soon began to earn quite simply bewildered him. To earn a lot of money was unarguably a good thing, in Peter Dormer's view. That Jack, who had idly frittered away his expensive years at Eton playing games and then amiably declared himself unsuitable for university, should yet fall on his feet, enjoying himself and getting highly paid for doing so, was hard to swallow. Peter's only consolation was that he supposed his own hard-working efforts to send the boy to Eton had got him into the old-boys network.

Penelope was his favourite.

But now, 'Darling,' said Lucy, 'Jack's bringing a girl down to stay.'

'A pretty one, I hope,' said Peter.

'Do you want to eat in or out?' asked Jack.

'Out, if you're hungry. You know Ma.' Henny threw her coat over the back of a chair. She was untidy. Automatically, Jack picked it up and hung it in the closet. Henny pushed her thick fair hair back. 'Pour me a drink first, will you, love?' Jack obliged. He didn't refill his own glass. He'd already had two and it was past 9.30. Not that that worried him, they always ate late. Henny took a grateful gulp. 'Lovely. Thanks. I needed that.'

'A surfeit of tea?' asked Jack sympathetically. Henny always went to see her mother at least once a week, after the day's work.

'By the gallon. Not to mention apple-cake . . .'

' "Eat it while it's warm".' Jack did indeed know Ma. 'How is she?'

'Fine. She's forgiven me for the washing machine. In fact she's wedded to it. If I'd stayed a minute longer she'd have had the clothes off my back.' Henny's ma, Marijke Brack, lived in a council flat in the East End of London. Even Henny, who wanted to give her everything money could buy, knew better than to try and shift Marijke out of the home she loved, the only real home she'd ever had. 'She's found an old lady who got out of Hungary the same time as she did, only much older.'

'So she's washing her curtains and making her goulash. Talking of which, I am starving. Come on. You can have just a starter.'

They made a handsome pair, strolling down Long Acre on a spring evening. The flat they lived in, one of the nicest in Covent Garden, was Henny's. Jack had sold his to move in with Henny; there was no contest between too far down the Fulham Road and this. As Henny was a star copywriter and Jack now an account director, their joint salaries put them well in the cashmere class. They had met at the advertising agency at which they both worked, Welbeck, Tannhauser and Streem. It was a very large, prestigious agency. To be there was to be at the top. To fall in love there was likely, a meeting of equals. To stay in love, to the extent of moving in together, was happily accommodated for Henny and Jack by the fortunate circumstance of their working on different accounts, he in his corner, she in hers and no acrimony.

Lucy Dormer swore she loved her children equally. But she knew it didn't worry her in the least that Penelope's fiancé, Brian Transom, was a bit of a bore and that it did worry her sick when Jack telephoned to say 'Mum, I'd like to bring someone home.' Chiding herself, she put her anxiety down to being like all mothers of sons.

'But of course, darling. Who?'

'We're working together. She's a copywriter. Well, more *the* copywriter. She's brilliant. And beautiful. She's half–Hungarian.'

'How exotic,' said Lucy, faintly.

'Not really. Her mother got out of Hungary somehow or other, when she was a young girl. Later on she married a chap called something Brack. A bit of a waster, I think. I don't really know. Henny's never even seen her father; her mother brought her up on her own. Can you imagine? Henny got to London University. She's brilliant.'

'Bring her, by all means. I'll look forward to meeting her.'

When they arrived at Alexandra Lodge for the weekend, Henny was pleased to find herself given the single guest room. Not that she didn't prefer to sleep with Jack but it wouldn't have been proper.

The only person privy to the impending arrival of Jack Dormer's young lady was Mrs Boxendale. Lucy had lived in Tiddingfold quite long enough to know which way to turn. She made up the guest-room bed herself, rather than ask Alma to do it. Apart from the fact that Alma despised blankets (Alma had duvets in her home), Alma also cleaned for Mrs Phillips the doctor's wife and Mrs Merritt the banker's wife, and a few other rising gossips. How she fitted it all in was explained by her brisk attention to tap-polishing and very little else.

'Jack's bringing a girl down,' said Lucy to Mrs Boxendale.

'Have a glass of sherry,' said Mrs Boxendale.

'I'm driving. But yes, I will. Thank you.'

Mrs Boxendale sipped her bumper of sherry and pushed the plate of unevenly cheesed salt biscuits towards Lucy. 'Why so gloomy? High time, I should have thought. If I were seventy years younger, I would have snapped him up myself.'

'She's clever.'

'So? You wouldn't mind that. You're afraid she's hard, aren't you? She probably is. Sit it out. Have another sherry.'

'No thanks. You wouldn't come to lunch on Sunday, would you?'

'Certainly not. I hate going out to lunch. I'd only get testy. And you'd be in a bother about me eating beef, which I can't chew, and the young lady would probably be charming to me, which I couldn't put up with. It's time for you to go, now. I am going to finish my sherry and watch the racing on television.'

Lucy left in higher spirits but, even so, in awe of this mysterious clever person who would be arriving all too soon.

'So it's you, Lucy,' said Mrs Boxendale at ten o'clock on Monday morning. 'Hang on a moment. The blackbird is sitting. I'm rather pleased. The wire netting I put round the nest hasn't fallen off.' It took her a few minutes to get seated and get her breath. 'Well, now,' she at last said. 'How is my young friend Jack?'

'Very well. Very well indeed.'

'Good. You seem cheerier today.'

'I am. Henny is a super girl. Oh, Cecilia, I do so hope they will get married.'

'And what about this cleverness?'

'Well, she is. But she isn't, also, if you see what I mean.'

'Not really. Perhaps you will explain.' Mrs Boxendale looked at the clock. Not yet time for sherry.

'Well, you know Heraclitus?'

'Jack's tortoise?'

'Yes. Only I have to tell you he's more mine, now, than Jack's. It's like that, isn't it, with one's children?'

'Betty,' said Mrs Boxendale thoughtfully 'has at least not landed me with any of her great lumping dogs. But go on.'

'Heraclitus is still really in hibernation. I've given him a box of hay in the garden shed. But Henny asked to see him. And, can you believe, she's working on a pet-food account and she'd brought down some special food. It's got cod-liver oil in it.'

'Very nice. And how did she get on with Penelope?'

'Fine, I think, though we didn't see much of Penelope. She and Brian were at a point-to-point on Saturday. They were in for Sunday lunch but they went somewhere straight after. But I think she likes Henny. I know Peter does, which I'm pleased about. Of course, she is very glamorous!'

In truth, Lucy hadn't the faintest idea of how her daughter felt towards Henny Brack. Penelope was in the business of being engaged and, as such, vastly superior to the whole world. Clever she may be, she thought, looking for flaws in Henny's beauty, but fancy! Twenty-eight and still not married.

3

About a month later, Jack brought Henny down to Tidding-fold again. This time, he took her to meet Mrs Boxendale.

Henny looked forward with curiosity to the meeting; Jack had spoken often and affectionately of the old lady. Now that Jack was in love with her and she with him, aspects of his boyhood fascinated her and Mrs Boxendale was a foundation part.

Her sitting-room reminded Henny, to a certain extent, of Ma's. Ma's table, china cupboard and ornament shelf were new, all having been bought by Henny. Mrs Boxendale's were old, inherited not bought. But both rooms were geared to a common main need: a comfortable chair and the television.

'Get the glasses, Jack, if you please. You'll take a glass of sherry?'

'If you're having one,' said Henny politely.

'Of course I am. But that is neither here nor there. One offers one's visitors sherry.'

Henny blushed. She seemed to have begun by making a gaffe. She wasn't sure where she should sit. Mrs Boxendale sank into her own easy chair and pushed the *TV Times*, a large-print library book and a pile of tattered magazines off a little table, in order to set down her glass. Henny perched nervously on the edge of a hard settle, remembering not to cross her legs. 'Well,' Mrs Boxendale continued, staring at Henny in the mannerless way of the very old, 'you're certainly good-looking. Lucy was right about *that*. I believe you're in the advertising business? I know little about it. But Jack seems to be making a successful career in it.'

'Yes indeed,' said Henny. 'That's how we met.'

'And you, too, are successful?'

'I'm afraid so,' said Henny, nervously fiddling with her necklace.

'What a silly expression: "I'm afraid so".'

'Sorry. Sorry, I don't mean sorry. Jack is an account director. I write the advertisements. You may have seen some on television.'

'I do not see the advertisements on television. I watch the BBC.'

Henny tried to smile placatingly but was too nervous.

Jack, long privileged to pour drinks in this house, filled Mrs Boxendale's glass. 'How is your blackbird?' he asked.

'The young have flown. How is your tortoise?'

'All right, I hope. I've neglected him but my mother is fond of him. How is Betty?'

'Very well, as far as I know. She has her dogs.'

Jack turned to Henny. 'Betty is Mrs Boxendale's daughter. She breeds dogs.'

'Are they nice dogs?' asked Henny.

'Nice?' asked Mrs Boxendale. 'I suppose so. For my own part, I am not very keen on dogs. Not all over the house. My father had some terriers and a labrador. He rode to hounds in Surrey.'

Henny leant forward. 'Did you like that?'

'It was not for me to like or dislike. I'm rather tired now.'

Henny was glad to leave. 'Thank you so much. I'd been looking forward to meeting you.'

Mrs Boxendale escorted her visitors to the front door, kissed Jack, shook Henny's hand and returned to her sitting-room. There she filled her glass to the brim and switched on the television. 'Hmph,' she sniffed, and selected ITV.

'She didn't like me, did she?' asked Henny, seating herself beside Jack in the car.

'What *do* you mean?'

'Well. I said all the wrong things. And she kissed you and only shook my hand.'

'Darling, of course she did. She's known me all my life and she's only just met you. She's an old lady. She wasn't brought up to kiss people the minute she meets them, the way we do. She probably only let her own husband kiss her after they were engaged. I wouldn't dream of telling her we're living together. She'd be horrified.'

Watching television and trying to work out which were advertisements and which programmes, Cecilia Boxendale mused to herself, 'Now I wonder if those two will get decently married or just go on living in sin. Won't make a lot of difference, Jack obviously adores her. Can't tell about her. Seemed a bit nervy to me. Very pretty, I must say. And she's got a nice mouth. Mouths tell. Your eyes you get, your mouth you make, I always think. He could do worse. As long as she makes the boy happy, that's all that matters.' She dozed off.

'I'm so glad you've been to see Cecilia,' said Lucy, when Henny and Jack got back to Alexandra Lodge for lunch. 'I'm fonder of her than anyone. She's been such a good friend to me. And she does so love Jack.'

'Yes,' said Henny, 'I can see that.'

Cecilia awoke on Monday to her usual morning stiffness of limbs. It would be nice to stay in her warm bed but she allowed herself no such indulgence. She almost tumbled on the way to the bathroom, but made it in time. Triumphantly washing her face with cold water, she returned to her bedroom, decided stockings were too much trouble and struggled into an old pair of Reginald's trousers and a blouse which she buttoned with care. It took a few goes not to run out of buttonholes. This achieved, she made straight for the garden, forgetting she had promised Lucy she would always take at least a bowl of All-Bran for breakfast.

May was gently giving way to June. The blackbird's offspring had found their way out through the chicken wire and had flown. The Albertine rose was covered with bursting buds. In the borders, the leaves of the Jacob's ladder stepped up in their orderly way, topped by the bunches of pretty blue flowers which would soon be fully out. She was content, and made her way into the house, contemplating a quiet hour before sherry. She had forgotten it was Alma's day.

'Oh, hell,' she thought, hearing Alma let herself in the front door in her noisy, bossy way. Alma had keys to every house upon which she bestowed her ministrations. Her attitude to

Mrs Boxendale was twofold. Mrs Boxendale fell indubitably into Alma's class structure, but she provided the added advantage of being old. Alma, born at the other end of Tiddingfold, had progressed. She had made her husband buy their council house and cover the front of it with imitation Cotswold stone. There were duvets on her beds, whether her husband liked it or not. She also fronted the day centre for the old folks, and was a great favourite with Mrs Phillips, the doctor's wife. At the day centre, she called the old dears by their first names but she still didn't quite dare to do so with Mrs Boxendale. For all this, on days when she found damp knickers stuffed down the side of the easy chair, she came within an inch of it.

'Well,' she said, breezing straight into the sitting-room, 'we do look down in the dumps.'

'Do we?' enquired Mrs Boxendale sourly.

'Let's just shake up the cushions, shall we?'

'You may.' Mrs Boxendale didn't move. Alma bustled about, removing an empty sherry bottle and coming dangerously near to knocking over Cecilia's favourite Copenhagen bird at the same time.

'The wedding's in June, then.'

Mrs Boxendale flinched as Alma flashed her duster about and moved the *TV Times* out of reach. 'What wedding?'

'Lady Lucy's, of course.'

'Lady Lucy was married thirty years ago.'

Oh dear, thought Alma, we *are* getting vague. 'I mean Penelope. Penelope, Lady Lucy's daughter.' She used her patient voice. 'Didn't you know? Haven't you been invited?' The heavily engraved invitation to the marriage of Penelope, daughter of Mr Peter and Lady Lucy Dormer, stood on the mantelpiece.

Alma had the effect of making Mrs Boxendale feel as if her skin was turned inside out. She had to sit very still. At last the woman got through with her flurries, biffed and disarranged the books with her duster, polished the bath-taps about which she herself couldn't care less, made a pot of tea and joined her with it. Mrs Boxendale disliked tea. But at last Alma's good works were finished and off she went, radiating complacency.

In the nick of time Lucy arrived. She saw Cecilia slumped

in her chair. 'Of course,' she said, 'it's Monday. Alma's been. She wears me out. She's well-meaning, though.'

'You're always so charitable, Lucy. Empty that damned teapot and get me a glass of sherry, will you? And, if you'd be so kind, go into the kitchen and get the biscuit box and see if there's any cream cheese in the refrigerator.'

Lucy knew where to look. She knew what tempted Cecilia as well as she knew the favourite snacks of the tortoise, Heraclitus. She emerged from the kitchen with biscuits, cheese and a couple of tomatoes which could have been fresher but were still edible. 'You met Henny?'

'Yes.'

'Come on, Cecilia. What's wrong? Don't you like her?'

'She's very pretty. Well, she's beautiful.'

'So what's wrong? I may as well tell you, they're going to get married. In a couple of weeks' time. In London. Peter and I are going, naturally. And I think it would please Jack if you were to come with us.'

'No.'

'But you've accepted to come to Penelope's.'

'That's quite different. I don't care about Penelope. Not that I don't wish her well, I'm sure her nuptials with young Brian Transom are suitable to a degree. I shall enjoy the champagne. I'm quite sure Peter will provide excellent champagne. But no. No, I don't think I feel able to go to London for Jack's wedding. I am too fond of him. All right, I'm sure she is a very nice young woman, if you think so. I just hope she makes Jack happy.'

'There's no earthly reason why she shouldn't. I hope they make each other happy. They've been together almost two years, so they know what they're doing. Won't you come? You know we'd be delighted to take you.'

'No, thank you all the same. It would be too long a day for me.' And that was final.

The following day, Tuesday, brought a surprise Mrs Boxendale's way. She was spending her usual morning hour out in the garden and had just tumbled over. She tumbled over quite often. Her greatest fear was that she might be unable to pick herself up before that dreadful Mrs Phillips woman should push her way through the side entrance with her, 'Halloo-oo, Cecilia.' But one advantage of Mrs Phillips's impertinent way of barging through the side and straight into the garden was that one at least knew it was her. Alma had her key, more was the pity. So when there was a ring on the front-door bell, Mrs Boxendale was willing to answer it. She beheld an apparition.

'Excuse me,' it said. 'But I was wondering, do you want your grass cut?' The apparition's hair stuck up like purple bulrushes. The face under the hair was white, with red on its eyelids. The hand on the front-door bell was furnished with mauve fingernails. The body between these extremes was clad in dusty black.

'Who are you?' asked Mrs Boxendale.

'I'm Maxine. I live down there.' A vague gesture towards the other end, the council house end of Tiddingfold.

'Why aren't you at school? On a Tuesday.'

'Didn't go.'

'So what brings you here?'

'Funny you should ask that. See, I can't see much in school. So I thought I'd like to earn a bit. And you've got a back garden and you're ever so old, aren't you?'

'So what to do you wish to charge me for this alleged service?'

'Alleged,' said the girl. It was a word she'd never heard. Mrs Boxendale was thinking she should back out. Alma had told her more than she wished to know about glue-sniffing in the council houses. 'What about a pound?'

'A pound an hour?'

'No. A pound for the job.'

'I'd want it done properly. In between the flowerbeds.'

'OK. Tell you what, then. Give me one pound first time. If it's all right and you want me back, you can give me one pound fifty. Got your own mower? I can use my dad's, if you haven't. But it's blunt. My dad's like that.'

The wedding of Henny and Jack took place shortly before Penelope's. Penelope was too busy with her own arrangements to attend it. In any case, Henny could hardly require her as a bridesmaid. At twenty-eight, her potential sister-in-law was almost middle-aged. In Penelope's view, it was obvious that

Henny would rush to get the ring on her finger first. Henny, Penelope noted, hadn't even an engagement ring. Hers, ponderously slipped on to her left hand, third finger, weighed a ton of diamonds previously worn by Brian's mother. The diamonds were not of the first water but that was neither here nor there.

'Are they Catholics?' whispered Peter Dormer to his wife. Lucy nodded and looked round the crowded church. Lucy was a little surprised that it was a church, not a Registrar's office, but she had reckoned without Marijke Brack. The church was full of expensive clothing but Lucy's husband and one other man were the only ones wearing morning suits.

When they had all gathered in Mrs Brack's small flat, the other morning suit came over and introduced himself. 'You must be Jack's mother and father. My name is Stanley Howard. This wine is excellent, isn't it?'

Peter nodded. It was, to his surprise, excellent champagne. When Lucy broke it to him that the reception was to be given by Marijke, his response had been 'Good God, sweet Bulgarian, I suppose.' Balkan geography was not his strong point.

'You must be a friend of the family,' said Lucy.

'It's the first time I've met Mrs Brack. I'm loosely what might be described as Henny's boss.'

'Are you Jack's boss, too?'

'No. I'm the creative director. Not that Henny needs much directing. She's an extremely talented lady.'

Peter Dormer left them talking and pushed his way to the other end of the room. Lucy smiled. 'He must have seen a pretty girl. Is your wife here, Mr Howard?'

'No. She couldn't get away. Our youngest is in bed with tonsillitis.'

'Poor little thing.'

Stanley laughed. '*Little* thing! Our youngest is eighteen and six foot one. But she's that sort of mother, bless her.'

Stanley saw Lucy glance towards her husband. Catching the glance, Lucy said calmly, 'Oh good. Peter's happy. He was a bit iffy about this reception. He's very conventional.' The girl Peter Dormer was chatting up was a secretary. She was, in fact, Henny's secretary. She knew who Peter Dormer was but he,

23

who couldn't hear too well above the noise, just enjoyed looking down her pretty cleavage while she was courteous even though longing to escape to younger company. This non-communication was just as well for, although Peter was glad his boy was marrying this clever, pretty girl so much liked by Lucy, he would have been thrown completely off course if he had been obliged to find her so much too clever by half as actually to have a secretary in her own right.

'Can I get you something to eat?' asked Stanley.

'Yes, please. I'm quite hungry. And the food looks wonderful.'

'Would you like salmon or risotto? I'm going to have both. I happen to know Mrs Brack's been cooking for the last three days.'

'I think I'm going to like my fellow mother-in-law very much,' said Lucy.

'Good. That's good. That's friendly. A good portent, I hope. How well do you know Henny, Lady Lucy?'

'Well enough to be already very fond of her.'

'So am I. I'm delighted she's married Jack, he's a great lad. Henny has a brilliant career in front of her.' Stanley looked at Lady Lucy. 'So has your son. So he has. Hope they make it.'

Marijke Brack had squeezed into a Crimplene costume for the occasion. She wasn't exactly fat but she had the one-piece look that comes from getting up too soon after having a baby and going back to work in a jam factory. Henny must have got her height and fairness from her absent father, Lucy thought. She followed Mrs Brack into the kitchen.

'Wonderful food, Marijke,' she said. 'I hope I may call you Marijke and that you will call me Lucy?'

Marijke poured herself a cup of tea. Lucy indicated that she would be grateful for the same. Marijke smiled. 'Yes. I would be happy to call you Lucy. I like your son. I am glad he has made marriage with my girl.'

'So am I.'

'I must tell you, I did not like this living together.'

'Oh, they all do it.' Penelope hadn't but then Penelope was Penelope. Lucy sipped the excellent tea. 'It should work out better in the long run. At least they know each other before they get married.'

'Living together is not marriage. I am old-fashioned, you see. I married. I married a bad man. I am sorry, my English is not good enough. He was not bad. He was not use . . . how must I say? Useless. That is the word.'

'Well,' said Lucy, 'you've got a lovely daughter out of it.'

The honeymoon was spent in Cannes. It was the perfect time of year. Jack had reserved a suite in the Martinez Hotel. They'd both been there before, to an advertising festival.

'Last time I was here,' said Henny, 'I went home with an award.'

'And this time you'll be going home with a husband.'

'Goodness, so I will!' There had indeed been a less than subtle difference in their arrival at reception. The time before, although she and Jack had been together, they had arrived as two delegates. Henny had signed in for herself. She remembered the reception manager, whose mask of impassivity concealed, he believed, his distaste for single ladies masquerading as businessmen in his hotel. He usually punished them by giving them equal bills for inequal accommodation. There had been quite a tussle on this score which had ended in a Pyrrhic victory for Henny. She got another room, little better than the first but could not be bothered to complain further.

But now he was all smiles and bows and welcomes. 'We have the best suite for Monsieur and Madame. We hope you will enjoy the flowers; they are with our compliments.' Henny behaved equally well, standing back with the correct invisibility while the manager obtained Jack's signature, man to man. The importance of wives, in his book, was how much their husbands would spend. He had no need to see wives' names written down. They should be young, expensive, able to read no more than the caviare side of the menu, and replaceable. His own wife was nothing of the kind. But she ran the shop up in Vence and banked money for his retirement.

The luxury was delightful. Lawn sheets, pale pink, not only on the double bed but also on a single bed nearby, perhaps in case of bridal modesty, or maybe for recovery from post-coital

25

exhaustion? A bathroom with enough equipment: gowns, soaps, toilet waters, shower caps and towels graded from face-cloth through to such vast things as could hardly be lifted off the rail. With these last you could dry two wrestlers and a horse, all sweating at the same time.

And then there was the ante-room, its tables concealed under linen cloths, velvet sofas, a refrigerator behind a screen in case the vulgarity of its purpose should offend. Not that its purpose was anything so low as something to eat. It was too posh even to contain the miniatures lesser establishments stocked. Champagne and more champagne. And then the balcony.

The balcony was what deceptive brochures would have you believe you'd get and then you didn't. But on this occasion, you certainly did. Wide, floored with pretence grass, it swept in a half-circle. You could see the sun come up, shade yourself at noon and then watch it set. Below it, the Mediterranean sea glistened and chuckled as though it knew what, whatever muck was washing up on its lesser coasts, this bit of it was lapping the well-swept sand exclusive to guests of the Martinez Hotel.

Henny leant over the balcony, a glass of orange juice in her hand. There had been so much champagne. Even on the plane the chief steward had brought champagne as the flight captain congratulated the happy pair over the Tannoy. Complete strangers had rushed up, enjoying the diversion and the bountiful booze. Couples bored to death with one another had patted and hugged the handsome couple in a happy fantasy of renewed youth. It had been talk, talk, talk.

Jack stood watching his wife, filled with love. The setting sun just touched her fair hair. He came forward and put his arms about her. Henny turned to him and stroked his cheek. 'How does it feel,' he whispered, 'to be a married lady?'

'Me?' asked Henny. 'You mean me?'

'Who else, Mrs Dormer?'

Henny considered her reply. 'Well,' she said at last, 'just the same, really. I'm still me, aren't I? And you are still you.' Jack took her hand and turned the wedding ring on it. It was a beauty. Solid gold, a little too large on her finger. As he restored her kissed hand to her, it almost slipped off. 'Do you think I should have it made smaller?' asked Henny.

'No. One day we'll be old and maybe your finger won't be so slim. Anyway, you shouldn't take it off. I love to see it there. And my grandmother, my father's mother I mean, always said it was bad luck for a woman to take off her wedding ring.'

Henny felt anxious. She had never heard of such a superstition. She knew she was careless with jewellery. She had some nice pieces, all of which she had bought for herself, usually items bought on a whim on the way back from lunch. Semi-valuable pieces seen in a window and quite affordable. But she was, and she knew it, careless with such easily acquired gewgaws and apt to leave them about. 'Oh dear,' she said now, dreading to hurt Jack.

'Don't worry,' he said. 'I'll see it doesn't slip off. We'll go shopping. I'll buy you another ring, to keep it on. How would you like a topaz? After all, I never had time to get you an engagement ring. I'd get you a diamond, but I know you don't like diamonds. You see, I know you so well. You're mine.'

The reception manager had reason and plenty to be pleased with Mr Jack Dormer. These were hard days. Such bounties as the easily handled film and advertising festivals of so few years ago were thinning out. His feet ached and he had to work harder. An English gentleman with money to spend was enough to make his *entente* pretty *cordiale*. A conference over the desk concluded with the arrival of a rented car and a rake-off. The rented car took Jack and Henny up to Vence to a little boutique of antiques, so charming. 'He knows the owner,' said Jack to Henny. The reception manager certainly did.

Jack, in his love, bought Henny a ring which she could not help but admire. It was indeed very pretty, and almost worth the phenomenal price Madame la femme de Monsieur le manager du réception au Martinez charged him. It was but the work of a moment for her to sum up a bridegroom in love, who wouldn't argue price in front of his lovely new wife. It was, she explained several times, a pleasure to do business with an English gentleman. It was indeed. The Americans always bargained.

'It's lovely,' said Henny. She was overwhelmed by the tenderness she was receiving.

Back at the hotel, she stood out on the balcony again, turning the topaz ring over the heavy gold ring.

In the morning Henny, sated with love-making, hardly heard Jack's suggestion. 'How would you like a house in Tiddingfold?'

'Love it. Go down every weekend.'

'What I really was thinking,' Jack started to say when a knock on the door interrupted him and breakfast was brought in. Henny never did hear what it was he had been about to say. The coffee was exquisite. French *café au lait*, the polite slap of water on clean sand, its reflection shivering across the ceiling, led to other things.

4

'You're back. Good. I need you,' said Stanley Howard. 'The pet-food stuff went through fine, so no need to worry about that. But we're pitching for Vara Cars. And I need your ideas, quick.'

'Cars?' said Henny. 'I don't know whether you realise it but I can't even drive. Do you think this is a good idea?'

'It's an excellent idea. Under the bonnet's for the manuals. Your bit is making people fancy themselves in the thing. Have a good holiday?'

'Honeymoon!'

'Oh yes, of course.' Stanley peered over his half-moon specs. 'Do they still call it that? Very romantic, I'm sure.'

'It was, as a matter of fact.'

'Good. I'm still calling you Henny Brack, with clients. That's how they know you.'

Henny wondered what Jack would have to say about that. He was so proud of calling her Mrs Dormer. She had not been used to hearing him speak possessively. She had almost laughed to hear him glowingly refer to her as 'my wife'. Well, she was. And happy to be.

They loved each other; that had begun very early on. Commuting two flats into one, which happened to be Henny's, had very soon become a practicable arrangement. Henny, in the offhand manner of those who are so businesslike they don't even realise they are, had bought the atticky place in Long Acre. When Jack got rid of the Fulham Road flat and moved in with Henny, the financial outgoings simply continued on Henny's standing orders. She had never been concerned about who paid for what.

She and Jack knew each other, heart, soul and body. When

he asked her to confirm their love by marrying, the formality held no terrors for her. Quite the opposite. She was proud to be so acclaimed. It would be the same but better. Being a husband increased Jack's stature. It had amused her to stand back, watching the manager of the Martinez signing Jack in and not even remembering the run-in she had given him before.

When Jack had bought the lovely topaz ring, his grand behaviour, his insouciant paying of what she knew was too much, good as the ring was, she received as a token of his love. She even had the tact not to buy him something in return. But she had been shaken at his anger over the business of the bill. At Jack's request, it had been sent up to the suite the day they were leaving. It so happened that Jack was having a shower when it arrived. Henny had opened the thick, crested envelope which contained its very large account rather as a crematorium contains grief in a chocolate-box wrapping. 'Goodness,' she said lightly as he came in rubbing his head, 'we sure put away a few oysters. Never mind, our credit cards are good as gold, thank heaven.'

'Please darling. Leave this to me.' Henny looked up. It was the first time she had heard him call her darling as though he didn't mean it. It was an enormous bill. He took it out of her hand and walked out on to the balcony, scanning it. She followed him. Somehow, she had hurt his feelings. And she didn't want to do that.

She put her arms round him from behind and tickled the place he liked to have tickled, just in front of his right shoulder. He moved away. 'I know it's cost a fortune, but hasn't it been fun?' she said, a little uncertainly and, she concluded later, obtusely, 'and anyway, we can afford it.'

'*I*', said Jack, 'can afford it.'

Now that he and Henny were married, Jack rapidly fell into the habit of digging her out of her office at going-home time. He was a lot more orderly than she. He never let meetings drag on. He took a tough line when they reached the point where someone would start in on such showings-off, as 'If I may interpret what so-and-so was trying to say'. It was Jack's opinion that the day was the day and anyone halfway efficient got things done by the end of it. Henny was a bit sloppy in this respect. She tended to go on, in the conviction that another go would make the ad better.

A few days after their return to work, Jack went to collect Henny. She was scribbling away at her desk. 'Come on, darling. Home time.'

'I won't be long. Give me half an hour.'

'I'll see you at home,' said Jack.

'I really won't be long. Why don't you go and have a drink in the pub with Bill and Charles? You like them.'

Henny was already looking down at her notes as Jack stumped out of her office. When at last she reached home, it wasn't difficult to see her husband was in a less than sunny mood.

'I'm home.'

No reply.

'Sorry I was a bit longer than I said. It's the new car account. Stan wants to present original colour names. I ask you, wouldn't you think white was white? But no, it depends whether we're thinking masculine or feminine. Stan thought winter-ski-white was masculine, so I said how about nappy-white for feminine? It's quite fun, actually.' She knew she was over-explaining. 'Shall we go out and have some dinner?'

'Can't we eat at home?'

Henny put her arms round her husband, surprised at herself for wheedling, but wheedling nevertheless. 'Tomorrow, promise. I'll go to Soho in the lunch-hour and get some food. Come on, darling, give me a kiss. After all, I was working, not out with another man.'

'I should hope not.' But Jack was smiling now. All was well again. Much later he said, 'If you want to go out to dinner, you'd better put some clothes on.'

Marijke Brack received a telephone call from her daughter, asking how to make goulash. Henny, having no idea of the complications involved, never having been present during the making of what she had always thought was an everyday dish, rang from her office. After several interruptions – 'Sorry, Ma, could you say that bit again?' – Henny gave up. She managed to rush out and buy, at enormous expense, a couple of fillet steaks. Unfortunately, she overlooked the need for potatoes and vegetables. The steaks had to go into the refrigerator. 'I'll try again tomorrow,' she said. 'I'm sorry. I'm just not used to cooking dinner. We've always eaten out.'

'We weren't married, then,' said Jack.

That Jack and Henny should come down almost every weekend to Alexandra Lodge was a great pleasure to Lucy. Her new daughter-in-law always arrived laden with exotic offerings: chocolate truffles from the shop in South Molton Street, ginger in a blue jar and packages of smoked salmon, always from Fortnum's. Henny, coming to a rurality she had never encountered outside of books, was unaware that smoked salmon was readily available and a great deal cheaper at any one of a large choice of the supermarkets scattered in or near every country town.

What Lucy most enjoyed was Henny's simple pleasure in the garden and the paddock. Penelope's superannuated pony still chomped grass surlily, unexercised and long forgotten by Penelope. Henny, who had never in her life been close enough to a horse to touch it, made friends with the creature, which took to following her round the paddock and nosing her.

And Heraclitus had come out from his hibernation. 'I don't know which I like best,' said Henny, 'the flowers or the tortoise. Isn't this a lovely rose?'

'I'm glad you like that one. It has a scent, you see. The modern roses often don't have scents. Mind you, they don't get greenfly.'

'Why's that?'

'Flies like scented roses.'

'Well, I never.'

These were happy weekends. Henny discovered that her mother-in-law was a good laugher. 'So tell,' Lucy would say, making salad.

They'd be in the kitchen. The reward of Henny's refreshing company negated what would have irritated her in anyone else: Henny's habit of always leaning on the refrigerator just when she needed the cream and on the oven when the pie was burning. Levered on to a tall stool, Henny would sip a glass of the white wine they usually shared while Peter and Jack were out being men, and start.

'Well, then, so Vara Cars. We got the colours right. I said women would like pink and Stan said I was being old-fashioned but I was right, so that was good. But then I thought I'd done a smashing headline. It went "The car a five-year-old could drive". I meant it was easy. But oh my word, the fuss. Well of course I wasn't suggesting that infants should pinch the car and go up the motorway. So I tore that up and got a picture of a pretty girl and headlined it "Even I can drive it." You can imagine, I got the politically correct wallop.'

They were now, on weekends, installed in the double-bed guest-room. It was a lovely room with a pretty view across the roses to the fields, but somehow not a room to make love in. It was private enough, with its own shower and bidet suite, and you could even get hot water if you ran it long enough (Alexandra Lodge had not entirely relinquished its ancient systems) but it was redolent of barristers. Even a circuit judge and his lady had pressed their persons upon the mattress. The only reason the circuit judge had brought his lady on the occasion was that Peter Dormer had discovered she was a distant relation of Lucy's. Lucy had absolutely nothing in common with her.

Henny and Jack drove down on a Friday evening. Henny usually slept in the car until she was woken, as the engine was switched off, by the song of nightingales. Saturday afternoon was cricket on Tiddingfold Green, Jack handsome in his white flannels, his father slightly squeezed into his. Lucy no longer turned out to watch; she considered she had graduated. But Henny did her duty. As long as there wasn't a cutting wind, she found it an enjoyable way to relax and an agreeable contrast with the working week.

Lucy was preparing for Penelope's wedding. There was to be a marquee, with silk drapes round its entrance, embellished with showers of flowers – miniature lilies, gypsophila and pittosporum, hanging upside down to match the flowers on the pews of the church. The flowers were to be ordered from Maison Fleur. Privately, Henny thought Lucy's garden flowers would be much prettier.

'I can't cook,' she confided in Lucy.

'Neither could I, when I was first married. But you don't need to worry too much about it. With both of you working, surely it's more sensible to eat out for the time being? I know I would.'

'We always used to. But Jack — he's so sweet — likes being at home now we're married.'

Lucy smiled. 'That's nice. Even so, I'd take the chance while I'd got it, if I were you.'

'I know,' said Henny, having a brilliant thought and paying no attention to Lucy's meaning, 'I know what I'll do. I'll get a cookery book.'

A couple of days later Henny's secretary, the pretty girl Peter Dormer had chatted up at the wedding party, buzzed. 'I have your mother on the line.'

'Ma! Are you all right?' Mrs Brack had never before rung the office. And it was more than two weeks since Henny had been to see her, which also had never happened before.

'I have an invitation. I don't know what to do. What means RSVP?'

'Oh I see. The wedding. Penelope's wedding. You'll come, I hope.'

'I don't like to. But such a nice note is in it. Lucy says I am to stay in her house. I never was in such a house. In such houses they all ride to hounds.'

'Whatever makes you think that?'

'Hello.'

'Hello? Are you still there?'

'Hello. It is in the doctor's waiting-room.'

'Oh, *Hello*! the magazine. Take no notice. Lucy asks you because she likes you. You must come down with Jack and me.'

For Penelope's wedding, Henny wore the cream-coloured wild silk suit she had worn on her own marriage day. It was a fraction too tight. She had given up smoking. Jack, who had once smoked about twice as many cigarettes a day as Henny, was now strongly against the filthy habit.

She was ashamed of a slight fear that Ma would turn up in bright blue splashed with pink flowers. She was even more ashamed to have so far forgotten Ma's intrinsic sense of what was proper. Mrs Brack, plump but dignified, wore plain navy and a small hat. Her only eccentricity was to spurn the florist's buttonholes and ask Lucy to give her instead a fresh rose from the garden.

It was Henny's first encounter with a Tiddingfold turnout. The church was packed. Maison Fleur, with such a large order to fill, had done the pew bouquets the day before and one or two of the miniature lilies looked a bit tired. A small bridesmaid who decided, halfway up the aisle, that she wished to bolt, knocked a bunch to the floor. But the organ pealed and everyone whispered what a pretty bride Penelope made. She had a curiously tanned look, having made up more for the photographers than for her own spiky little face.

Jack, so handsome in his morning suit, proudly introduced his own bride to all the guests. There was plenty of time to do so. Before the reception line, which took an hour in itself, even started to move, the photographers had their day. Outside the church, getting in the car, arriving at Alexandra Lodge . . . it went on for ever. Henny longed for a drink.

'Mrs Boxendale, you've met my wife, haven't you?'

Mrs Boxendale was leaning on an ebony stick. 'Yes. Tell me, is your real name Henrietta?'

'It is. But I've been called Henny for so long.'

'Very well. You're a little plumper than when last we met. Never mind, it suits you.' Mrs Boxendale was longing to sit down. But she hauled herself upright.

'Dr Phillips. Mrs Phillips. My wife, Henny.'

'You must be glad to get out of London,' said Mrs Phillips. 'Isn't this a lovely day? Penelope, such a beautiful bride.'

'Yes, indeed. Isn't her dress pretty?' said Henny.

'Quite lovely. It will be an heirloom. I heard it cost more than £1,000. But Peter and Lucy dote on her.' Mrs Phillips, Henny could see, was paying her quite a lot of attention. It crossed her mind that, had she been a lesser object than the daughter-in-law of the Dormers, Mrs Phillips would have been looking over her shoulder in search of more important personages.

'Major Blunt. Mrs Blunt. My wife, Henny.'

Henny shook hands. Mrs Blunt, whose shoe-heels were

getting stuck in the lawn, looked as though she needed a glass of champagne as much as Henny now did.

But movement was taking place. 'Come along, darling, we must go and join the reception line.'

'Us? You didn't tell me,' said Henny.

Jack seized her elbow and pushed past the waiting guests. Inside the marquee, she could see Lucy and Peter. Lucy was elegant in a coffee-coloured outfit of couturier cut. 'Marvellous what you can get from Oxfam,' she told Henny cheerfully. 'But don't tell Penelope.'

Henny stood beside Jack at the end of the line. In centre place stood Lucy and Peter Dormer and Mr and Mrs Transom with, between them, the bride and groom. Penelope received kisses on her cheeks. Enough photographs had been taken for her to allow the makeup to be touched. Brian Transom stood a pace behind his bride, whose day this was. She scarcely looked round at him. He had, after all, already been adequately photographed.

Henny became aware that someone was nudging her. ''Ere,' hissed a voice. 'You don't half look tired. Want a glass of wine? You're allowed. They're nearly through.'

'Who are you?' asked Henny.

'I'm Maxine. They've got caterers and all but Lady Lucy said I could help out. She's going to pay me. I've met your mum. I'm nosy, me.'

'How do you know she's my mum?'

'Don't be silly. I know everything what goes on in Tiddingfold. That Mrs Phillips, huh. Your mum's nice, isn't she? Foreign. Posh, that is.'

'She's not posh at all,' said Henny. 'Neither am I.'

'Well, I know that. It's just like, it's exotic. Makes a change, in Tiddingfold. Don't like Miss Penelope much. Do you?'

'Just give me the glass of wine,' said Henny.

Now at last the reception line was concluded. The guests began to drink the champagne provided by Peter Dormer and to nibble the caterers' fingers of asparagus quiche and the hard pastry-cases with soggy contents.

Maxine kept bobbing into Henny's direction. 'You met Mrs Boxendale?'

'Yes.'

'She's all right, Mrs Boxendale. I go to her. When you come to live here, I could help you. If you would have me.'

Henny looked at Maxine. She was wearing a tight black skirt, so long it would have impeded the movement of her legs but for the split up the back. Her white shirt was crisp. Her hair was a cockscomb. 'That,' said Henny, 'would be very nice. But I don't think it will be very soon.'

Maxine went off on her duties. She filled Mrs Blunt's glass for the third time. She liked Mrs Blunt. 'Hang on, this bottle's empty. Give me a tick,' she said. Bumping into Henny at the buffet, she said, 'Don't forget now, if you want any jobs done when you move in.'

'When I move in? What do you mean?'

'Have I got it wrong? I heard you was coming to live in that house in the high street. Three doors up from Mrs Boxendale.'

'Oh?' said Henny.

'Oh yes. It's all over. Everybody knows. Oh dear, I shouldn't of said. Jack, you know, well, your husband, I expect he meant it to be a surprise. I wish I had a boyfriend like him. He's ever so good. Everyone says so. My dad heard in the pub. He's bought that house. Mulberry Cottage. My dad says it's falling down but my dad says things like that. He would, wouldn't he?'

The wedding party went on and on. Henny longed for a cigarette but steeled herself. Instead she drank more champagne and began to feel aggressive. She decided the only sane thing to do was to avoid a confrontation. His sister's day was hardly the time to berate her husband for going out buying houses behind her back. Tomorrow, she thought, I'll ask him about it tomorrow. But when tomorrow came, she changed her mind. It was for Jack to tell her.

And he did. 'I've got a surprise for you, something to show you,' he said, the next weekend.

Mulberry Cottage was so pretty; a dream of a country cottage. Henny loved it on sight. 'Are we going to buy it?'

'That's the surprise. I've bought it already. It's for you.'

'I don't know what to say,' said Henny. This was true. To have said, 'You might have asked me first,' seemed petty in the

37

circumstances. Even more so since she had fallen in love with the place, which clearly proved how well Jack knew what she liked. She looked down at her topaz ring and remembered his unerring comprehension of her dislike of diamonds.

Lucy and Peter greeted an ecstatic Henny on the couple's return to Alexandra Lodge. 'Jack's bought a weekend cottage, I didn't know a thing about it. Can you believe it?'

Peter Dormer could believe it very well. His first reaction to Jack's interest in the place had been, 'The boy's a fool. No surveyor would pass it; I wouldn't lend a halfpenny on it and he certainly won't get a mortgage.' But when he discovered the price he had to admit that his more-money-than-sense son had found a bargain. Mulberry Cottage, languishing under probate, its ancient owners long dead, was a snip. In a few years, properly done up, who knew what it would be worth?

He put a fatherly arm round his daughter-in-law. Now that she looked like nesting she didn't seem quite so daunting. He was quite astute enough to have taken in her phrase '*weekend* cottage' but dismissed the prefix as a towny description of a country home. And for all her elegance, she was endearingly soft to the touch. He looked at Jack with new-found respect. A wife with sex appeal *and* brains. Good outlook for the next generation of Dormers. He decided this was worth a bottle of Moët.

Lucy, whose attitude to champagne was rather like Henny's to diamonds, was happy to see Peter pleased but asked him if he wouldn't mind getting a bottle of the Bulgarian red, since it was only shepherd's pie for lunch.

Lunch went off well. Peter was particularly pleased with the cheese Henny had brought. It was more stylish than sturdy and the grape-pips got between his teeth. But, all in all, he liked the girl and could settle down on Saturday afternoon to watch the rugby.

Henny and Jack returned to Covent Garden on Sunday evening. The heating had not turned on as programmed. They went to bed.

On Monday morning, Lucy went to see Cecilia Boxendale. 'Jack's bought Mulberry Cottage,' she said.

'Yes. Maxine told me.'

'They'll be using it for weekends.'

'Oh?'

'You're very testy this morning, Cecilia.'

'Am I? I don't feel very well.'

5

Stanley Howard was slightly annoyed with Henny Brack. As far as he knew her husband, Jack Dormer, he liked the chap. Couldn't blame him for loving Henny. Couldn't blame Henny for loving him. Couldn't blame either of them for committing marriage. Stan's own marriage was as happy as could be. Sylvia. Sylvia who was perfectly happy to use her capable brain in her own home. He wouldn't have it any other way. Their way was satisfactory.

He had not expected that Henny Brack would start to leave early on Friday afternoons. 'I'm going down to Tiddingfold,' she announced.

'I see.'

'Don't be grumpy, Stan. I'm happy.'

'Great.'

'I've left the Vara Cars copy on your desk. I want to catch the two o'clock train. We're doing up the cottage and Jack wants me to get down before the builders finish for the day.'

'Why you? Why not Jack?' He knew he would get an evasive reply and he did.

'I'll be in early on Monday morning. If you want any changes to the copy, leave them on my desk.'

'All right. Not that I expect to need changes. I don't usually, with your copy. Can't think why you young people have to have country cottages.'

'It's only a weekend cottage.'

'So far. Oh well, have a nice time and don't get pregnant. Off you go.'

As good as her word, Henny was in early on Monday morning. By half-past eight she was at work. An hour later, Stan found her working on the Vara copy, looking slightly puzzled.

'Sorry, Stan, I read your note. I don't know how I came to forget the heated rear-windows. I've got it in now. Look.'

Stan picked up the copy, not remarking that he also had been slightly appalled. 'Yes. That's fine. I'll get it off. Have a nice weekend?'

'Lovely. Absolutely lovely. The cottage is . . .' Henny paused and then continued. 'Stan. I say, Stan, are you free for lunch? On me?'

'You know me, never a man to turn down a free lunch.' Stan's heart sank. 'Where are we going?'

'Rules. OK?'

'There's posh. It isn't every day a pretty lady takes me to Rules.'

Typical Henny, thought Stan, to be able to make them give her the best table in the restaurant. She'll find it a bit of a change, if she's about to tell me what I think she's about to tell me.

'Have the duck, I am,' said Henny. She pressed him to eat a starter as well. Stan had no objection, being a hearty eater and drinker and priding himself on his unique triumph as the only long-lasting member of the agency with neither an ulcer nor a weight fad.

Henny ordered the same but picked at it. Ah-ha, thought Stan, off our food, are we? So what's coming?

'Stan. I say, Stan.' The second time this Monday she'd said 'I say'. Not like her. He remained silent. 'I want to ask you something. Tell me about Sylvia.'

'What do you want to know? These potatoes are good.' Henny's glass was still full; Stan's was empty. But the waiter, with whom Henny was a favourite, soon remedied that.

'You've got children, haven't you?'

'Mm-hm. What have you done, you bad girl? Isn't it enough that you forgot all about those heated rear-windows without sitting there, elegant as can be and two days pregnant?'

'No, I'm not.'

'That's a relief.'

'But Stan, the thing is, I'm going to resign.'

'Oh shit. There's no such thing as a free lunch. I knew it. Can I have pudding? You owe it.'

'You know the cottage? Mulberry Cottage?'

'I haven't escaped. Yes, I'm aware of Mulberry Cottage,' said Stan. 'I'll take a glass of port, since you press me. Go on.'

'Well. We bought it for weekends, as you know. But when I got down there on Friday, the builders were just leaving and they'd taken out the old windows but the new ones hadn't arrived and they hadn't even tacked plastic over the frames. And they hadn't done half the things they were supposed to do. They said they couldn't get on with the kitchen because I hadn't decided on the flooring and they'd thrown out the old wash-basin from the bathroom, which was the nicest thing in it and . . .'

'Go on. No. Don't. If you want to know about Sylvia, the reason we live in great comfort in Bromley is because, twenty years ago, she got behind the builders and drove them with a whip. Damn it to hell, what am I saying? Oh Henny, why did you do it? Why couldn't you just have gone on living with Jack? I know you love him and it's clear he adores you. You didn't need to spoil it all by getting married.'

'Stan, look at you. You're the only calm man at WTS. And Sylvia is happy, isn't she?'

'Sylvia isn't you. She isn't a career woman, never wanted to be. My darling Henny, you've worked so hard to get where you are.' Stan drained his glass of port. Accepting another, he braced himself and continued. 'Right then. I suppose you've got to give it a try. I'll let you go. Tight, taught, tractable.'

'So for all I forgot about the heated rear-windows, you liked my Vara Cars headline? I must say, I thought TIGHT, TAUT, TRACTABLE was pretty good myself.'

'I'm tight. God knows what you've been taught and I don't like to see you tractable. But there we are. Better have a cup of coffee before we stumble back. What are you going to do about your flat?'

'I'm not sure. I thought of putting it on the market. I won't be earning, which doesn't matter. Jack earns enough for both of us. And he got the cottage as a bargain. Even so, he hasn't quite realised how much it's going to cost to make it liveable. If I sell the flat, I could make it really gorgeous. Open up the attics, put in central heating, make another bathroom . . .'

'Oh shut up, Henny. If you're going to do what I plainly see you are going to do, let it be Jack's affair. Keep the flat. You might like to come to town for a matinée. Or to see your mother.'

'Good idea. Actually, you're quite right. You know, Stan, one of the best things about going to live in Tiddingfold is that it's bringing Jack and his father together again. Peter, my father-in-law you know, was always a bit disappointed in Jack. Jack never said so, he wouldn't. But I've picked it up. I like my father-in-law. He's a self-made man.'

'What about your mother-in-law?'

'Lucy? Ah, Lucy's something else.'

'So you like your father-in-law and you love your mother-in-law.'

'Right. Tiddingfold is going to be a great new experience. Jack is very fond of an old lady called Mrs Boxendale, who lives three doors down from Mulberry Cottage.'

'Oh God, meals-on-wheels time.'

'Stan, I'm very happy. I've never gone in for marriage before. And I am much loved. Don't you understand?'

'I'm trying to. But why? What's it all about? What does he expect you to do all day? Coffee mornings? Amateur painting groups? And have you thought what it's going to be like, not having your own salary?'

'Sylvia doesn't.'

'Different. Quite different. So keep the flat. For the matinées. I've finished my coffee. Do we go back to work or do we go on to Soho and get seriously drunk?'

September celebrated Henny's new life. She was sure she had done the right thing. She woke up on her first Monday morning, turned over in bed and found no Jack. So Jack had become an early riser. She stumbled down to the kitchen and looked round to see if she could find an egg. If her husband was going off to work, he ought to have an egg for his breakfast. Her own mother had always sworn by an egg on toast for Henny's breakfast, before school. She put the kettle on to make coffee and it immediately steamed up the window. She rubbed a sleepy hand over the glass and saw Jack, out in the garden among the weeds. Maybe Lucy or perhaps Mrs Boxendale would be able to explain to her what one did about weeds.

The high street was empty as Henny kissed Jack goodbye on the front doorstep of Mulberry Cottage. She wandered through the empty house and out into the back garden. It was long, narrow and tangled with rank grass and the remnants of long-ago flowers gone feral. Beyond and below, threads of mist were slowly rising in the field that sloped away. Season of mists and mellow fruitfulness. Henny shivered and turned back indoors.

Jack hadn't had a very good breakfast. She had lived two years with Jack without their ever having breakfast together. From the moment they got out of the bed that dominated their shared pleasure, each of them had attended, in silence, to their own arrangements for the day.

To be fair, on this first morning, Jack had brought her a cup of tea. At a quarter of an hour short of seven o'clock. If Henny liked tea at all, which was not much, it was her mother's tea. Strong, in a glass, with lemon. This milky stuff almost made her sick, especially as it was cold, but she swallowed it.

Henny called Jack in from the garden for his breakfast. 'Boiled egg, good.' He topped the egg with his spoon and peered inside. 'Oh. Well, never mind. I never did like hard-boiled eggs.' Henny looked with disgust at the revolting sight of clear, raw white of egg.

'I'll do you another. Oh dear, there isn't another. Let me scramble it or something.'

After Jack had left, belching burnt scrambled egg, Henny washed the breakfast dishes sadly. She rinsed everything meticulously. People could get allergies or even madness from detergent left on dishes. Or so she had read. Then she made the bed. New percale sheets and Witney blankets. She had never before heard of Witney blankets and now found they were so heavy she had broken two fingernails before she was through. But they were what Jack wanted, having grown up under them. Then she got out the vacuum cleaner. The vacuum cleaner was quite distressing: it seemed to blow instead of suck. One thing to write advertisements about these things; quite another to use them.

Exhausted, Henny decided to break off and read the news-papers. She didn't expect to find an orderly pile of them in the sitting-room, the way they had always been in her office. So she went down to the village shop. It was only 9.45, though by now it felt a lot later. But the village shop had no *Times*, no *Daily Mail*. 'The *Telegraph*?' she asked.

'Oh no. Everyone has their *Telegraph* on order. I can't afford to have any left over.'

'The *Daily Mirror*? The *Sun*?'

'Wouldn't think you'd want *them*. The council houses have them.'

'Well,' she said, 'I'd like to place an order for papers, daily. *Times, Independent, Daily Mail* and *Mirror*.'

'*All* of them?'

'Yes, please. You deliver?'

'No. People collect. If you want to order all those – '

'I do. And the *Observer* and *Sunday Times*.'

'. . . you'll have to pay for them.'

'I didn't expect not to. Presumably weekly payment will do?' Henny looked with distaste at the stout woman behind the counter. 'Have you got a nice chicken?' she enquired.

'Buxted. Frozen.'

'Don't you have farm chickens?' She got a look of unmiti-gated scorn. Ruffled and depressed, Henny picked out a frozen chicken pie and one of those green tissue-paper lettuces, the tissue paper gone limp and faintly yellow. Its price was 87p. Ma would have had a fit.

Back home, she looked round the kitchen. There was no washing machine. There was no dishwasher either, come to that, but she had never thought about dishwashers before. Between Ma and the soft-footed Filipino woman who did all the work in the Covent Garden flat, Henny had had very little domestic experience. She telephoned her mother-in-law.

'Lucy? Are you busy or can you come to my rescue?'

Henny was full of her day when eight o'clock brought Jack home. 'Your mother took me into Ashden. I've ordered a washing machine. And a dishwasher. They're coming next week. She's been so kind, your mother. She was really amazed when I said I couldn't drive. But I said I'd never needed to, what would I have done with a car in Covent Garden? Anyway, she said we could put that right straight away and she took me to get a provisional licence. She's going to teach me herself and then she says I must have some lessons, so as to pass the test. And it was so funny with the Hoover, and . . .' she suddenly realised that Jack hadn't listened to a word she had said. She had hoped he would be pleased. 'Oh, I'm sorry, you must be starving.' She went into the kitchen.

The outside of the bought chicken pie was burnt and the inside was still frozen. The lettuce had been wilting for hours, in a very unpleasant dressing, also bought from the village shop. 'How was your day?' asked Henny, having left the question too late.

They went to bed. Jack made love in a husbandly way. It was quite nice, Henny told herself, to be a married lady with a husband home from a hard day at the office. She responded staidly.

Fortunately, this had its effect upon Jack. Suddenly he was wide awake. 'What's got into you, girl?' he enquired.

'Not much, now you ask. I thought it was the way you wanted to do it.'

'It was. But we've done it. So now let's do it properly.' They ended up rolling and laughing, and happiness was restored.

Next morning found Henny more confident. Nice to know one can be a married lady and still have a good time in bed. She bought a box of eggs and boiled them one by one, holding in her hand the stopwatch she once had slung round her neck when recording voice-overs for commercials. By a process of elimination, she managed to work out that the way to make the perfect soft-boiled egg was to put it in cold water, bring it to the boil and then time it for exactly three and a quarter minutes. Emerging from this experiment heady with the excitement of it all, there was just one more thing. What did one do with six eggs in various stages of composition?

She looked forward with enthusiasm to Jack's return. Meanwhile, the egg business having taken all morning, she had another go at the vacuum cleaner, after which she took a long bath, got lavish with the Byzance (full strength, not mingy toilet water) she had bought in the duty-free shop on her way back from the honeymoon, and attired herself in slippery silk. The garment could only be described as deceptively simple. Any fool thinking she could buy a couple of yards of stuff and run it up would be the more deceived. The way it fell round Henny's slim body had to do with its costing the kind of money she had so airily spent before she changed her life.

Hearing Jack at the door – he always ran the engine for ten seconds before he switched off; he was kind to cars – Henny dropped the *Times* crossword to greet him. He surveyed the pile of newspapers, spread all over the floor. She gathered them up. She knew she had never been tidy; Jack was the tidy one. 'I ordered them from the shop. You have to order,' she said.

'We're going to have a hell of a bill.'

'I suppose we are. I hadn't thought of that. Have a drink?' She had remembered to get ice out. Jack would want a gin and tonic. She'd even got a lemon. The ice had melted. Damn, she knew there was something. She should have put the lid back on the ice bucket.

'What is this?' asked Jack at the table she had nicely laid.

'Oh, a little something.' It was the remains of the eggs. Unfortunately, the village shop only had Kraft slices, which didn't seem at all like fresh Parmesan. The pastry wasn't a smash hit, either. Unwilling to try her own hand, Henny had accepted a packet of frozen flaky from the grim-faced fat woman.

'Couldn't you get steaks? They're easy,' said Jack.

'There's no butcher in the village,' said Henny, prodding her own soggy portion with little enthusiasm. 'I'll ask your mother where she goes.'

This evening, she did not ask Jack how his day had been. And hers was hardly worth telling. They watched the ten o'clock news. 'Early start tomorrow,' said Jack. They didn't make love. Well, last night had been enough. Jack snored. He had never snored before he was a married man. Henny patted his back lovingly.

At about half-past eleven the next morning, unable to think of anything else to do in the house and with a week to wait before the washing machine and dishwasher would be delivered, she took a walk up the village street. The newspapers she had collected at 9.30, but somehow her brain didn't seem keen enough to take in their contents.

Walking past Mrs Boxendale's house, she saw the old lady in her little front garden, on hands and knees under the white rose bush. 'Good morning,' said Henny.

'Good morning,' said Mrs Boxendale, rising with the slow dignity she was obliged to adopt, on account of her legs being well behind her brain.

'I was just passing.'

'I don't wonder. You must be bored to death with living in Tiddingfold. Did you really want that house?'

'Jack did. I love it. I've never lived in a house before. I grew up in a flat, you see.'

Mrs Boxendale, now upright, gave Henny a searching look. 'Oh well. You're young. At least I see you are putting in some decent windows. There are people in Tiddingfold who will tell you a lot of rubbish about how you mustn't change them. I put in plastic frames. I hope you are doing the same if you are planning to live in the place.' She swayed a little and Henny restrained herself from putting out a helping hand. At last steady, Mrs Boxendale continued: 'Would you like a glass of sherry? And before you feel obliged to enquire as to whether I wish to have one, I most certainly do. Come in.'

Entering the sitting-room side by side with her muddy-handed hostess, Henny wasn't sure what she should do. It was all right for Jack, confidently familiar in this house. She hovered. Mrs Boxendale fell into her chair. 'Would you,' asked Henny cautiously, 'allow me to get the glasses?'

'Well, of course. Hurry up.'

'Of course. I just thought I wasn't supposed to.'

'You aren't. But I'm falling apart. Not the Tio Pepe, the Amontillado.' Mrs Boxendale held her glass in both hands, took two deep breaths and a deep draught. 'That's better. Now. About this house business.'

'It'll be lovely.'

'Jack must be mad.'

'But I thought you were so fond of him?'

'I am. I wish he'd consulted me. Buying this house, without even asking you. Wrong thing.'

'Maxine said it was a lovely surprise.'

'Maxine's a romantic. I say this is all wrong for you.' She saw Henny looking puzzled, and added, 'You seem surprised I should say such a thing.'

'I am, actually. I would have thought you'd be pleased to have Jack living almost next door. Perhaps not me, so much, if you don't think I'm the right kind of wife for him.'

'I never said that.'

'I know. But it's fairly obvious.'

Mrs Boxendale laughed aloud. 'Oh dear. What an awful old woman you must think me.'

'I don't, as a matter of fact. I think you're very strong and I like strong people.'

'You wouldn't have thought me so strong if you'd known me when I was your age. What my husband ordered, I carried out . . .'

'Jack doesn't *order* . . .'

'. . . And lived to regret it. We had to, in those days. It was a different world. One was lucky to get a husband. The war, you know. I was not attractive, in the fashion of the day. To tell you the truth, I never thought I'd get married. And it was a disgrace, not to. It's quite different nowadays.'

'Up to a point. A few months ago, I never thought about marriage. Jack and I were happy together. It was my flat we lived in. And then, when he wanted us to get married, I was pleased. Apart from anything else, my mother is old-fashioned. She didn't like to have her daughter living in sin. She still called it that. Everyone thinks council flats are full of crack and single parents on the scrounge. But where my ma lives, they're very respectable. So anyway, I'm married. And I'm jolly well going to make it work.'

'Good for you. You just happen to have jumped a fence without giving a thought to what was on the other side. Have another glass of sherry.'

'Aren't I staying too long?' asked Henny. 'Don't you want to have a rest?'

'If we are to be friends,' said Mrs Boxendale in measured tones, 'I will ask you to have the kindness never to suggest that I need a rest. I shall, eventually, rest in the grave. In the meantime, let me see. How fast the morning has gone by. Now that's an odd thing. At my time of life one finds that the years go faster than one would wish but the days, in the ordinary course of events, go tediously slowly. If you have nothing better to do, perhaps you would care to join me in a snack. I live on snacks. It is one of the benefits of being a widow.' She heaved herself up out of her chair. 'I have some Philadelphia cheese in the refrigerator, and some rather nice biscuits in a tin. I get them at the shop.'

'That woman in the shop,' said Henny, following her.

'I know,' said Mrs Boxendale, 'she's quite awful. She once stopped supplying my newspaper because I had forgotten to pay the bill. My late husband wouldn't enter the place. But it suits me. I need so little, in the way of food. I get my sherry by the crate. Dear Lucy arranges it for me.'

'She's wonderful, isn't she?' said Henny.

She got a searching look from Mrs Boxendale. 'Yes. She is. And I'm happy to observe that you mean what you are saying.'

Henny and Mrs Boxendale were watching the racing on television. It was the first time Henny had ever sat in front of a television set in the afternoon. Having drunk three glasses of sherry, she was unconscionably dozy. Mrs Boxendale, as soon as she had instructed her young friend on the colours and running of the elegant creatures with their long brown legs, closed her eyes happily as Henny murmured how like dancers were the delicately balanced jockeys in their pretty silks.

Mrs Phillips, hell-bent on doing good, elected this moment to make her way – 'Halloo-oh!' – into Cecilia's back garden. Mrs Merritt tagged along. They were to go later to a garden centre. 'Just look in on old Mrs B., I can't help but be a little concerned about her,' Mrs Phillips had said.

'There's someone looking in through the window,' said Henny. She recognised Mrs Phillips and jumped to her feet like a guilty schoolgirl, rushing sherry glasses and crumby plates into the kitchen just as Mrs Phillips and Mrs Merritt barged through the back door.

'Don't disturb yourselves,' said Mrs Phillips, shoving her way into the sitting-room.

Henny couldn't find the television control. The horses had long been re-boxed and replaced with a rackety cartoon of extreme violence, cats, dogs and mice smashing one another into walls and ceilings. Mrs Phillips took a skilful look around and announced in an awfully sweet voice that she would go and make a pot of tea. 'How nice,' said Henny, feeling quite insane but longing to get the woman out of the way.

Mrs Boxendale looked like a collapsed rag doll. But Henny now had her first experience of finding what the old lady was made of. By the time Mrs Phillips reappeared, Mrs Boxendale was upright. She managed, without speaking a word, to convey her opinion of people who entered one's home and made tea without being asked to. To Henny the message was loud and clear; even Mrs Merritt looked slightly uncomfortable. But not Mrs Phillips.

'Shall we have the TV off?' Mrs Phillips would have turned it off had she been able to find the control.

'I am watching this programme. It is a favourite of mine.' Mrs Boxendale hung on firmly until the end of the cartoon, after which she reached into the mare's nest beside her chair, disinterred the control and switched off. 'I take it,' she now said, 'that you are paying me a call.'

' "Paying a call" – ' Mrs Phillips explained to Mrs Merritt, who did not know the old lady as well as she did. 'Paying calls would be a memory of when she was young.' She spoke as though Mrs Boxendale was deaf as well as old. And, as a matter of fact, Mrs Boxendale didn't hear the remark. She was concentrating on how soon she could get rid of these people. Mrs Phillips patted Mrs Boxendale's gnarled hand. 'You know Mrs Merritt, don't you?'

'I believe so. Are you not the wife of the bank manager?'

'And you know me, too, don't you?' Mrs Phillips interrogated.

'Well of course I do. You came here when you married the doctor. Weren't you a nurse or something? Funny how doctors always seem to marry nurses.'

Mrs Phillips smiled firmly. It was a fact that, long ago, a crisp uniform, a fairly pretty face and a coat-holding, instrument-handing demeanour had won her the reward of marriage to Dr

Phillips. This reward was now in full bloom. Her children grown up, she had become the proprietress of the Elms Nursing Home, an establishment furnished with scrolled carpets to conceal elderly spills. The Elms was doing modestly well. Geriatrics thrived in Tiddingfold. But recruiting was perpetually essential. And a gem such as Mrs Boxendale – thanks to her friendship with Mrs Merritt, Mrs Phillips was privy to Mrs Boxendale's substantiality – was worth netting.

Mrs Merritt rose to the occasion, looking round Mrs Boxendale's sitting-room as she spoke. 'You must have been very happy, here.'

'*Have* been? I *am* happy here.'

'Oh yes indeed – ' slightly routed, but not entirely – 'it's a charming house, of course. But don't you sometimes feel a little lonely? Without your dear late husband?'

'My husband has been dead for over fifteen years. I could hardly feel lonely now if I didn't then. And as you see, I have a new neighbour. Do you know Mrs Dormer? She has just moved in and today I invited her to lunch.' Henny almost burst out laughing at the emphasis on the word 'invited'.

But it was lost on Mrs Phillips. 'And you have your daughter,' she doggedly continued.

'I seldom see her. She has her own life. Wouldn't you expect her to?'

'So who looks after you?' Mrs Merritt had her eye on Mrs Phillips. The Elms Nursing Home was a big account at the bank.

'I have a cleaning woman. You know her. Alma.'

'Yes, Alma's excellent, of course. But a couple of mornings a week is not what I call "looking after",' said Mrs Merritt.

'Far from it. But I have also acquired the assistance of a young woman called Maxine.' Mrs Boxendale smiled to herself as both ladies tut-tutted.

Suddenly bored, Mrs Boxendale rose from her chair. Crossing the room, she tottered. But she achieved her intention, which was to show Mrs Phillips and Mrs Merritt out.

'Did you smell her breath?' Mrs Phillips curled her trained nurse's nose. 'Drinking.'

'And the room. Dust!' said Mrs Merritt.

'More than dust. There's incontinence coming on there, or I'm no judge.'

They drove away to the new garden centre. It had just opened and they had heard it specialised in miniature fuchsias for hanging baskets, and patio roses.

'I saw Mrs Boxendale today,' said Henny to her husband that evening.

'Did you? Good,' said Jack.

'She asked me in and invited me to stay for lunch.'

Jack gave her an approving smile. 'You're honoured. Apart from my mother, there aren't many people she'd ask in. It's a compliment a lot of them would give an arm and a leg for.'

'I hadn't thought of it quite like that. But,' Henny giggled, 'I take your point. Mrs Phillips and Mrs Merritt turned up. She certainly wasn't best pleased to see them.'

'I'm glad she likes you.'

'I'm glad I like her. And you'll be glad to hear that dinner is not another chicken disaster. I dug a couple of lamb chops out of the old bat at the shop. And your mother gave me some nice young runner beans. So give me a kiss and let's eat.'

'I saw your friend Stan Howard today. He was asking after you.'

'How come you were talking to him? You don't work on the same accounts.'

'Went to the Red Lion for lunch and he was there. He was a bit stiff at first. Seems to think I've immured you. I must admit I do want you all to myself.'

'Immured me? Was he pissed?'

'A bit, I suppose.'

'You said "at first". Then what?'

'He went back to work. He always does. But after his third drink he asked if I loved you enough.'

'And what did you say?'

'Oh, I said you weren't too bad.'

'There's eloquent!'

' "Enough", indeed. I love you more than I could ever say;

53

you're my whole life. You can't believe what it means to me that you're so happy here. You are happy, aren't you?'

'Yes, indeed. Very.'

'Then there's just one more thing. Don't you think it's time we thought about a baby?'

Henny was taken aback. Of course people wanted children. She did herself, she'd be quite unnatural if she didn't. 'Are you sure you want one so soon?' she asked hesitantly.

'It wouldn't be all that soon. By the time you've come off the pill, I mean it doesn't always happen straight away, does it?'

'I don't know. I've never enquired.' But from the way Jack spoke, he must have been thinking and hoping.

'And we've got a proper home now. We're all ready for it.'

'I suppose so. It's a big responsibility. See, I've never had anything to do with babies. I'd be scared I didn't know what it needed.'

'You would,' said Jack trustingly. 'Anyway, you've got your ma. And mine too. Oh well, let's not get too solemn about it. Tell you what, since you're not off the pill yet, let's have one for the road.'

6

Penelope Transom paid her sister-in-law a short visit towards the end of October, to announce the exciting news that she was expecting a child. 'What about you, Henny?'

'Not yet,' said Henny, refusing to be put about by Penelope's complacence. 'I've got enough to do with trying to learn to cook food fit to eat, not to mention passing my driving test.'

'You'd better not leave it too late. I know it's fashionable for career women to put off having children until they're almost forty. But you're not a career woman now, are you?'

'Neither am I almost forty,' said Henny, in as pleasant a voice as she could muster.

Penelope, who was already walking pregnant, rambled on condescendingly. 'I'd like mine to have a little cousin. Will you have a nanny or an au pair? We'll have a nanny, I got on to Norland the minute it was confirmed. Frightfully expensive, I know, but personally I wouldn't have anyone not properly trained. Still, different people have different ideas. You might not like to have a Norland nanny.' Her unspoken words – you grew up in a council flat, I know you're clever and all that but at least I know what's what for the sort of child we expect in *our* world – hung in the air between them.

'We'll see,' said Henny and added, 'I'm very happy for you, Penelope. I hope you feel well?' Oh Lord, why had she asked? Now she was treated to a blow-by-blow description of morning sickness, the exact second when the invisible creature was supposed to wriggle in its bath of amniotic fluid and how to avoid swollen ankles.

After Penelope had at last left, the vicar called. He had come as a bit of a surprise to Henny, who had the vaguest of notions – mostly literary, and nineteenth-century literary at that – about country vicars. This one wore socks inside his sandals, had one of those beards that looked as if he'd forgotten to shave and he spoke in designer cockney. 'Hi,' he said breezily. 'Hi, Henny.' Henny had no objection to being called by her first name but she did wonder what Mrs Boxendale thought about it. 'Just looked in to ask your help,' the vicar continued, 'with the parish mag.'

Well, thought Henny, it would be something to do. Maybe an article about a townie finding her feet in kindly Tiddingfold. 'Could be fun.' She picked up the vicar's breeziness. 'What would you want? A one-off piece, or were you thinking of a regular column?'

'Not exactly. We've got all the writers we need, and more. Everyone can write. No, what I had in mind was typing. Miss Smithers, Gladys, always used to do it, she was a typist at the council offices. Dear soul, so faithful to the mag for years after she retired. But she's too arthritic now, alas.'

'Oh dear, I'm sorry. I'm afraid I can't type.' This was quite untrue: Henny had always typed her own copy, rapidly and accurately. The vicar looked surprised. Well, thought Henny sourly, if you want to be a trendy vicar and disappoint me when I'd been expecting a nice old gent with a proper collar and one of those black chest-apron things gone green, it's high time you learnt all working girls aren't somebody's typist. Having been mean, she softened and offered him coffee, which he drank with a great deal of sugar and half the contents of the biscuit tin. The chocolate ones, not the plain Maries.

Intoxicated on caffeine and chocolate, the vicar dug into his sincere mind to find something for the newcomer. Involvement; so important. 'What about meals on wheels?' he came up with.

'Sorry. Can't drive. I'm a bit useless, I'm afraid.'

'No one's useless,' said the vicar. 'Anyway, we can talk about all that sort of thing later. Splendid news about Penelope, isn't it? We need some christenings, Tiddingfold was getting a bit elderly. May I hope we can look forward to another, in the not too far distant future? Jack is so popular and of course everyone in Tiddingfold wants to make you welcome as well.'

Jack enjoyed commuting. Nowadays, he had the happiness of

leaving home well breakfasted. Henny had learnt to boil an egg and make toast-soldiers. He was already on 'good-morning' terms with the other train-catching husbands. Some of them exchanged anecdotes of their toddlers' precocities. One in particular liked to tell of the lip his two-year-old son had given his mother. 'So put your shoes on,' the mother had said. 'No, you do. You lady, me man.' Even as he laughed along with the carriage full of husbands, he privately resolved that no child of his would ever speak to his darling Henny in that manner.

It wouldn't be long now. As soon as the prescription was finished. Loving Henny as he did, he paid attention to what she said and it seemed that the female metabolism had to be given time. You couldn't just throw the pills away. It all had to be done in the right order. And he read an article in the *Telegraph*, which he secretly preferred to *The Times* because its sports coverage was better, which said that the most fertile time for conception was just after stopping the pill.

Every now and then there would be a hold-up for a bomb warning at London Bridge. It made a man think about the future. Jack found it rather exciting. Henny safe at home, himself out in the dangerous world; protector, hunter, bread-winner.

On this particular morning, his train was late arriving in London because the driver hadn't turned up at Ashden.

The receptionist of Welbeck, Tannhauser and Streem had long legs and a charming manner. 'I'm sorry, he's not here yet,' she said, smiling at Mr Kevin Preston-Jackson, who had announced that he had an appointment with Jack Dormer.

Kevin Preston-Jackson smiled back, his charm equalling that of the receptionist. He had been out of a job for a long time. He had sent, to Jack Dormer, a well doctored c.v.

He looked impressive. A bit on the old side, thought the receptionist, but the coat was camel hair. 'Can I get you a coffee?' she enquired.

'Thanks. Got the *FT*? Left early this morning, missed mine.'

'The newspapers are on the table.' The receptionist forgot the coffee. Kevin Preston-Jackson picked up the *Financial Times*. Then he picked up the *Sun*.

'Got to read everything, in this business,' he said, in case the receptionist should think he was a *Sun* reader. He needn't have bothered. She wasn't listening. Someone else had come in and taken her attention.

By the time Jack hurried in, reception was full of arrivals. The receptionist, her desk-telephone tucked into her shoulder as she dealt with all-comers, favouring them impartially with the smile she prided herself on, waved an indication towards Kevin Preston-Jackson.

Kevin had finished the *Sun* and got through the *Daily Mirror*. But it didn't take him a second to see that Jack Dormer was a man who was flustered by being unpunctual. He was right.

'Sorry I'm so late,' said Jack. 'Trains. No driver.'

Kevin looked at his watch, composing his face into an ingenious expression which conveyed that he quite understood but hadn't time to waste. He accompanied Jack to his office, subtly ushering him in as though *he* were doing the introducing and making sure to give Jack no time to hang up his coat, never mind have a pee.

Jack fumbled through the papers on his desk. At last he found Kevin's c.v. 'You do realise,' he said apologetically, 'that it is an assistant I am looking for.'

'I know what you mean,' said Kevin, genially. 'No blinking. I'm ten years older than you.' Twenty would have been nearer the truth. 'But I've heard so much about you. And, to be perfectly honest, I need a job.'

'Of course, I see. Your last agency was PTV. They went out of business, didn't they?'

'Under-capitalised. I did tell them, but what can you do?'

Perusing the c.v., Jack now said, 'This is interesting. I see you were at Beaumont's, six years ago. You must know my wife. She was there at that time.'

Kevin tried to remember the dollies of Beaumont. 'Who was she?' he asked guardedly, hoping he hadn't pinched the wrong bum.

'Henny Brack.'

This was a bit of a hiccup. That bitch, Brack! Too clever by half. 'Let me think,' he said. Oh yes, I can just remember her. Where is she now?'

'At home. In Tiddingfold. She's left the business. We decided to move out of town. She's having great fun. Country life is new to her. She loves it.'

'Isn't that nice!' said Kevin. It was, indeed, as far as he was concerned.

He left the office a man with a job. The salary was measly but he was in no position to quibble about that. He went off to have a drink and put a bet on the 2.30, already working out how he would make up the deficit. He was an expert in putting in his expenses.

As Kevin went out, Jack's secretary came in. She rather liked the look of Kevin. Distinguished, hair grey at the temples and the sort of collar and tie to give a girl confidence.

Her name was Glenda. She had not been sorry to see the departure of Henny Brack. Glenda wished to rise to executive position and her way of doing it was to emulate the pilot-fish, which feeds off the leavings of the shark. Not that marine biology was any part of Glenda's concern. Simply, Jack was her meal ticket, so far. 'Is Kevin Preston-Jackson going to join us?' she asked.

'I have offered him the job,' said Jack.

'That's nice,' said Glenda. 'I'll be working for him as well, then?'

'Do you mind?'

'Not at all. I'll just hang your coat up. You do look tired. Your train was late, wasn't it? The pet-food meeting has begun. There's a lot of them come in. I've told them you'll be there as soon as you can.'

The pet-food meeting went off only moderately well. Jack arrived in time to hear the brand manager pecking at the copy. He glanced enquiringly at Stan Howard, who was listening in silence. It was never Stan's way to be defensive. But it was his way to present the creative work with an assurance that hardly ever failed to induce confidence in clients. Today, that air was missing.

Afterwards, he said to Jack, 'Not one of our better efforts, I fear.'

'You were very quiet.'

'Didn't know what to say. The stuff isn't up to scratch.'

'I thought it was all right.'

'All right, yes. But not brilliant. To put it bluntly, not Henny.'

'Give your new chap a chance. He'll get it together in time. They seemed all right at lunch. Look at it this way: some clients rather like feeling a bit creative themselves.'

'A well-known way of making lousy ads,' said Stan gloomily. This was clearly not the moment to complain to Jack what a loss was Henny's departure. She knew the account. She had a brave and original approach. The new chap was going for awards and showing every sign of not being up to the awards and not down to paying sufficient attention to the commercial facts. 'Give Henny my love and tell her I miss her,' he said.

As it turned out, Stan's message was not passed on to Henny. Nor did she learn of Kevin Preston-Jackson's infiltration. She could see that her husband was tired. He, suffering from indigestion after too large and too long a client-lunch, roused himself to apologise for not eating the dinner she had cooked.

Henny had gone to some trouble. It had taken her most of the day and a lot of anxious chopping. She was on the verge of telling the boring tale of how she had rejected the wizened tomatoes and picked out the good ones, but had the sense to shut up. She removed the dishes to the kitchen where she remained, overwhelmed by an intolerable longing for a cigarette.

The following Sunday, Lucy Dormer gathered her family round her for roast beef and blackberry and apple pie. It was a crisp day, with a nip in the air to remind her she must soon prepare the tortoise's hibernating box. Heraclitus, who knew all about the seasons, would follow her into the wood-shed and inspect his winter quarters, peering in as though to assure himself that the decor was up to last year's standard.

Peter Dormer smiled round the table as he carved the beef. He never tired of this ceremony and Lucy always ordered the beef to be taken off the bone and rolled. Carving was a man's privilege that meant a good deal to Peter. He liked to sharpen the knife on the steel, usually the wrong way round so that he blunted it. Hitting the bone would infuriate him, and Lucy liked Sunday lunch to be a pleasant experience for all. Leg of lamb was out of the question.

Peter took charge of conversation. Lucy, who was fond of her husband, always enjoyed this bit. He was apt to be a little facetious but at least he spoke, which was more than his father had done on the long-ago occasion when Lucy had been entertained to her first meal with her in-laws, an experience best forgotten. An effort had been made in her honour but Peter's mother had hardly sat down, clearing plates almost before the knives and forks were laid down, and darting out to wash up between courses.

She could see Peter mentally selecting suitable subjects. Now all she had to think about was not forgetting to warm up the pie.

'Well, my boy, and how's the ad-biz?'

'Fine,' said Jack. 'Busy week, actually. Interesting, though. I can't complain: seem to be flavour of the month just now.'

'Glad to hear it. Bit early to hope for a seat on the board, I suppose?'

Henny was pleased to see the dignity with which Jack settled this parry. 'Don't ask me that yet. You know me, I go one step at a time.'

'But it's coming, then, is it?'

'A seat on the board, you mean?'

'Well, of course I do. My dear boy, I'd be the first to admit I don't know a thing about your business. But I do know two things. If you don't create your own partnership, which is what I have done – ' Peter Dormer looked towards his wife for acclamation, which she would have given if she hadn't been busy serving the vegetables – 'you've got to have a seat on the board.'

'Give me time. I'm extending my team, for a start.'

'Sounds all right. Yes, I can see that. I was never a one for big companies myself. But I see what you mean. It shows who you are. So what have you got? This extension.'

'I've got a new assistant.'

'Excellent.' Peter genially swallowed his second glass of claret. 'Got a good chap?'

'I believe so. Took quite a brave step, actually. The guy's quite a few years older than me.'

Henny looked up but made no enquiry. She would have

61

liked to know who Jack's new assistant was, but had rapidly picked up the order of the day, so remained silent.

Her turn came. 'Well, young Mrs Dormer, how are you settling into Tiddingfold?' Peter had decided to like Henny. His son had certainly picked a looker.

'Very well, thank you.' Henny sidestepped her curiosity about Jack's new assistant and paid attention to her father-in-law.

'Funny lot, Tiddingfolders. A bit slow to take to newcomers. But hearts of gold, once they do take to you, hearts of gold. Just a question of fitting in. Anyway, you look well on it. Put on a bit of weight, I see.'

'So has Penelope,' said Henny, tight-lipped. Just as she thought she was doing so well . . .

'Ah-ah. She has indeed. And are we to learn the same good news of you?'

'No. That's not the reason. It's because I gave up smoking.'

Lucy tried to catch Peter's eye. She was glad Henny had quit smoking but she herself would have been dragged at the cart's tail before she would have mentioned the few pounds gained in the struggle. Whether Henny was trying to become pregnant or not she did not know either, this being another topic upon which she would not have the impertinence to enquire.

Fortunately, attention was now riveted on Penelope, who had gone into full-scale maternity kit. She wriggled on her chair as though she already had piles. 'All right, darling?' asked Brian. He was a booby, which didn't matter on account of his rare quality, which was having lots of money behind him. And he was a decent booby, now elevated to the dignified position of expectant father. The more fretful Penelope became, the prouder he felt.

'You're in it up to your neck now, Brian,' said Peter. Although he considered himself to be fond of his daughter-in-law, he was not all that at ease with her. But with Brian he was quite comfortable. Peter's rise to wealth and position in Tiddingfold was based on the patronage of Brian's forebears, good with a gun but half-witted when it came to reading the small print, or any print at all outside of *the Field* come to that. Brian now sat at his table, an assurance that this satisfactory generation looked like being perpetuated for a safe while longer. Peter was indeed comfortable with him, indeed genial. 'Didn't take you long, did it?'

Brian, feeling quite a one, was equally content with his father-in-law.

Lucy brought in the pie and cream. Henny accepted a helping. She would have preferred to refuse but shuddered at the prospect of her kindly father-in-law's 'Dieting, are we?'

After coffee, she went out with Lucy to see the tortoise. When she came in, Jack was ready to go. He was waiting by the car. 'I'll walk, if you don't mind,' she said.

'It's getting dark.'

'Not yet. You go on. It's only a couple of miles. And I like looking over the hedges.'

She watched the sun go down. Strange, how brilliant its colour was, the colder the evenings became. How sharp the shadows, how red the berries, how silvery the old-man's-beard.

When she reached home, Jack was asleep in front of the TV. She looked for the Sunday papers and eventually found them, neatly stacked on top of the dustbin, ready for Monday morning's collection. She brought them back into the sitting-room and scattered them over the floor, deliberately and resentfully. 'Why did you throw the papers out before I'd seen them?' she said loudly.

Jack woke, with a look of surprise. 'I'm sorry, darling, I thought you read them this morning.'

What a stupid fuss she was making, getting touchy about nothing. She pulled herself together. 'I had a lovely walk, coming home.'

'What?'

'Me, walk! It was lovely. You should take more exercise yourself.'

Jack licked round his dry mouth and pulled himself upright. Henny was being bossy, on his behalf. He was pleased. 'Happy, darling?' he asked.

'You know I am.' Henny went into the kitchen and made a pot of tea.

Jack roused himself. 'What about bed?' he asked.

'It's only half-past five,' said Henny.

'I wasn't thinking about bed for sleep.'

'I was going to read the papers.' Henny looked at the muddle of pages and made an attempt to tidy them up. 'Sorry,' she heard someone say. 'I know I'm untidy. It must infuriate you.' She sat on the floor and leant her head against Jack's knees.

He stroked her hair, murmured 'I love you whatever way you are,' and flipped the control to another channel.

Henny saw one of her own commercials come on. 'Oh,' she said. 'Look. That's the last pet-food one I did before I left.'

Later she made more tea and some sandwiches. The TV flickered on through a load of codswallop. When Jack said, eyes drooping, 'Got to make an early start, beddy-byes for me,' she remained downstairs, to lock up. It was only ten o'clock when she made her way up to bed. She hoped the light by which she read would not disturb him.

She patted his shoulder. She loved him. She should have acceded to his request to make love in the afternoon. After all, there wouldn't be much chance of that sort of jollification once a little Dormer or Dormers were old enough to open doors. She would have liked to wake him but thought perhaps better not, since he had to get up so early.

He turned over in his sleep, dragging all the bedclothes off her. Carefully, so as not to disturb him, she managed to pull back her share of the sheets and the Witney blankets. The nights were getting chilly. And Henny was filled with an unaccountable depression.

7

'I did it to spite that Phillips woman,' said Mrs Boxendale, puffing on a cigarette. 'But now, I have to say, I enjoy it for its own sake. Very consoling. Quite clears the head, especially of what the head wishes to be cleared of. Have one?' she offered Henny the pack.

'No. I'd love one, you can't think how much. But no, thanks. I don't want to go through giving up all over again.'

'Giving up,' snorted Mrs Boxendale. 'Giving . . . the nicest word in the dictionary. Giving *up* the most depressing phrase. Have a glass of sherry. Go and get the glasses, will you?'

'I'm honoured.' Henny went to the big old corner cupboard, now known to her.

'Just get the sherry,' said Mrs Boxendale, 'and tell me what you've been up to.'

'Never a dull moment. We went to lunch with Lucy and Peter on Sunday. Roast beef and blackberry and apple pie.'

'It always is; the only thing dear Peter can carve, and Lucy wouldn't have it any other way.'

'Well, it was very good. Crisp on the outside and pink in the middle. I must remember to ask her how long she cooks it. Good pie, too. Mind you, I could have done without my father-in-law pointing out that I've got fat.'

'Nonsense. You're just as thin as you were.'

'He wanted to know if I'm expecting.'

'Peter never had any tact.'

'Oh, he's just pleased about Penelope . . .'

'. . . who is wearing maternity garments like a tent, I notice. How's Lucy's tortoise?'

'Going into hibernation. She was getting his winter quarters ready.'

'She's inordinately fond of that creature. Odd taste. But then, she seems to be fond of me, so I can't complain.'

'You were very kind to her when she first came to live in Tiddingfold. She's told me.'

'Was I? I forget.' Mrs Boxendale brushed aside the accusation of kindliness. 'So, apart from luncheon at Alexandra Lodge, how else are your days filled?'

'I had a visit from the vicar,' said Henny.

Mrs Boxendale chuckled. 'Oh, him, poor fellow. All socks and sweetness, such a ditherer. His own conscience says he's in favour of female ordination and all the time he's looking over his shoulder at Tiddingfold. His conscience wants to take him to Canterbury. Bad luck to land in Tiddingfold on the way. Can't fill the church here and can't get to Canterbury unless he does.' Having disposed of the vicar, Mrs Boxendale continued, 'So how is my friend Jack?' Her sherry glass was empty and she became snappy. 'Following in his father's footsteps, it seems to me. I once thought he had more imagination.'

Henny rose to Jack's defence. 'He's doing very well. He has hired an assistant. I don't know who, but he seems pleased with him. I'm sure he's made the right decision. But he doesn't talk much about work by the time he gets home.'

'That's what I mean. Here he is, with a clever wife who knows all about his business and he doesn't talk about it to you.'

'Oh, I'm out of it now,' said Henny lightly. She didn't want to think about it and she didn't want to talk about it. And she couldn't think of another topic and she didn't want to go home where there was nothing to do but there ought to be. She was sure other wives were busy all day.

Mrs Boxendale was wondering if Henny wanted to go but didn't know how to, and Henny was wondering if Mrs Boxendale wanted to be rid of her but was too polite to say so. In the awkward silence this dilemma caused, the doorbell rang and in came Lucy.

Lucy had already looked in at Henny's house but did not say so, or why.

Sunday's lunch had gone off well; it always did. Lucy usually only half listened, her life was like that. Family, pleasantness and then, with any luck, an hour or so to herself to read. She had long ago despaired of understanding challenging books and stole moments to retire, as though to a secret vice, with her ancient E. Nesbits and Juliana Horatia Ewings. It was hard to understand why this particular Sunday gathering had left her anxious and depressed. Why shouldn't Henny elect to walk home rather than go with Jack in the car? It was a good idea: Henny was learning to love the countryside and, as Peter had not failed to point out, had put on a little weight, so to take some exercise was sheer common sense.

Penelope and Brian had stayed on. Brian was thinking of taking up golf and it gave Peter, Lucy realised, pleasure to think it was he upon whom his old-family son-in-law depended to be allowed to play his way in. Peter was a good golfer. While Peter and Brian talked golf, Lucy, pretending not to be longing for her privacy, had suggested to Penelope that she should come outside and visit her ageing pony. 'It's too cold,' Penelope had said. 'I feel the cold dreadfully now.'

At last they were gone. Lucy stacked the dishwasher, a mindlessly soothing task as long as Peter didn't do his well-meaning thing of offering to help, which meant piling up a few plates with squashed remnants of vegetables and meat fat stuck between them and putting them in the sink in cold water. She never snapped at him.

By the time all was cleared away, Lucy, realising that this restless evening was not going to be assuaged by escape into the lives of Victorian children, went out to Heraclitus's shed. It had grown dark. She took a torch. Hovering at the edge of his box, the tortoise blinked in the wavering beam of light. The torch needed a new battery. Lucy squatted down beside him. 'What do you think about it all, Heraclitus?' she asked. Heraclitus, in his infinite wisdom, did not reply.

So a day or two later and not really knowing what she was worrying about, Lucy drove down to the village and looked in at Henny's. It was but a step on to Cecilia's.

She was received with such a welcome that her spirits shot up.

'Lucy, dear, how nice to see you! Henny and I have just

been having a glass of sherry but maybe you will join us in another.'

'Why not?' Lucy wanted to hug Cecilia. Her anxiety lifted as she realised what it had been about. Simply, the fear that Henny wouldn't be able to endure Tiddingfold. She wouldn't blame her, God knew the place was full of bores, bores who thought themselves and their preoccupations fascinatingly interesting. She was used to it and had become, without even being aware of it, a talented escaper. But Henny's arrival had suddenly and disturbingly sharpened her focus. Even in the short time that Henny had been her daughter-in-law, she knew she would miss her dreadfully.

'We were talking about the vicar,' said Henny.

'Poor vicar,' said Lucy.

'Funny about the vicar,' said Cecilia, livening up at the prospect of another legitimate glass of sherry. 'As soon as his name is mentioned, someone says "poor vicar".'

'That's awful, isn't it?' said Lucy. 'But he's in such a stew, what with female ordination or not and I can't even work out whether he's for or against.'

'And who cares?' asked Cecilia. 'I always went to church when I was young and Reginald always went. He liked singing the hymns and reading the lesson. I used to think I'd like to read the lesson but he would have had a fit. He liked the old vicar. But yes, this new chappie, poor vicar. They don't know where to put themselves, do they? They'd be out of business if it wasn't for women applauding God and arranging the flowers. Oh well, the Church has gone to hell on a hand-cart and that's that!'

'He asked me to help with the parish mag,' said Henny.

'He's had one good idea, then,' said Lucy. 'You don't mean to say he's looking for someone to write something interesting, for the first time in history?'

'Not exactly. He wants it typed out.' Lucy was appalled at the insult but Henny, seeing her face, added, 'Maybe I shouldn't have been so stuffy about it. I've got to do something. I'm not much use, am I? Meals on wheels, for example and I can't even drive.'

'You will very soon,' said Lucy.

'There's going to be a Christmas bazaar. I saw it on the church noticeboard. They want cakes and jam, stuff like that,' said Henny without much enthusiasm.

'Believe me, darling, Mrs Phillips and Mrs Merritt make excellent jams and marmalades. And cakes. I don't compete.'

'Oh, dear. Boiled eggs and toast-soldiers, that's all I'm fit for. Honestly Lucy, I feel completely useless.'

'I never heard anything so silly in my life. Jack adores you.'

'But I ought to do something,' said Henny.

'Give a party, then,' said Lucy, suddenly inspired. 'The people here love parties and most of them are too mean to give any more than a bag of twiglets and a thin gin. If you want to make your name, and I can see you do and I can see why, give a party with the best food they've ever had.'

'Boiled eggs and toast-soldiers?'

'Get your mother to come down. I'd love to see her again, anyway. Come on, cheer up.'

'Has Heraclitus gone into his box?' asked Henny.

'He seems to like it. He hasn't quite settled. He still comes out for something to eat. He'd like your boiled eggs. He's very keen on the top of a boiled egg.'

Henny felt more cheerful by the minute. The wheels of country life, she reflected, ran very much more smoothly when oiled by large glasses of Cecilia Boxendale's Amontillado. She even felt brave enough to agree with Lucy that yes, she should give a party.

For the first time in weeks, Jack managed to catch the 5.58 train home. Kevin Preston-Jackson was proving invaluable. Although he had had two or three wives, he had none just now and was willing and able to work late. And Glenda had come up trumps. She looked after Kevin as assiduously as she looked after Jack; even more assiduously, in fact.

On the train, Jack fell asleep. But he awoke refreshed and was pleased to get home and find Henny looking prettier than ever. She told him she had seen his mother that morning, and Mrs Boxendale as well. She served him stuffed pimentoes. He had had stuffed pimentoes at lunch, first course. But he did not say so.

Before he could switch on the television, Henny made her announcement.

'I'm going to give a party.'

'Good.'

'A big one. I don't want to be ostentatious, but your mother says that a party with really good food would please people.'

'I'm sure it would. Well done, darling.'

Henny decided on written invitations. Cards that had AT HOME printed in the middle, under and overlined. The stationer in Ashden was willing to charge her for having *Mrs Jack Dormer, Mulberry Cottage, Tiddingfold* printed at the top. 'If you go for a thousand, you'll save money,' he said. Henny agreed, pushing aside the horrifying thought of the years and years of Tiddingfold parties it would take before they'd be finished.

Acceptances rolled in: 15 November was the date.

'Ma?'

Marijke Brack heard a note of panic. She had just settled down to watch *Neighbours* when the telephone rang. She liked *Neighbours*. The people in it were richer than her own neighbours, and the sun always shone. Nevertheless, they seemed to have some of the same problems as her friends who lived on the landings of her tower block.

'Ma?'

'One moment. I switch off. So, what's the trouble?'

'I'm going to give a party. With food.'

'So I'm to make the food? All right. I'll have to make it in your kitchen.'

'That's what I hoped you'd do. Lucy sends her love. She looks forward to seeing you. Thanks, Ma. I don't know how to give a party.' She could hear her mother sighing.

'I educated you to be a big success. And now you tell me you don't know how to give a party.'

'I never did. I took people to restaurants.'

'I shall come on the train. Tell me the day.' Marijke had once taken Henny, as a child, on a day excursion to the seaside. Otherwise, Henny's holidays had consisted of school trips, for which Marijke paid with teapot savings. The day excursion had been her one and only train journey. But now that she was necessary, she spoke in the tone of one who usually flies Concorde.

The day before the party, Lucy drove Henny to Ashden to collect Marijke. It was as well, she thought, as she watched Marijke get out on to the platform, that there were two of them. The guard had to wait to blow his whistle while Marijke got back into the train three more times to fetch out plastic bags, some of which seemed to be leaking. Marijke made a final return, to shake hands with a young man who handed out the last bag.

'Ma,' said Henny. 'I said a party. Were you planning on the guests staying all week?'

'Careful with that torte,' said Marijke.

Lucy grabbed a trolley and wheeled it out to the station yard, laden. 'The torte is the right way up,' she said, ushering her fellow mother-in-law into the front seat.

'Your country is very lovely,' said Marijke, as they left Ashden behind them. 'So much colour.'

'A lot of leaves have fallen, I'm afraid. We get such fierce winds here.'

'By now, in my home country, would be snow. What are those berries?'

'Hips and haws.'

'Hips and haws?' Marijke filed the knowledge. 'Ah, and that is holly. On the tree. Where I live now,' she shifted from the past to the present, 'I see it only in bunches. On the stalls, for Christmas. Here it is free?'

Henny carried her mother's suitcase up to the bedroom she had prepared. Marijke made straight for the kitchen. By the time Henny came down, she and Lucy were drinking tea, Marijke prowling and poking, cup in hand. 'What,' she enquired 'is this?'

'A microwave.'

'Ah,' Marijke peered at the thing. 'I have heard of these. A lady I know says they give cancer.'

Henny wasn't mad on the thing either. But she'd been per-suaded to buy it by the salesman who had seen his opportunity the day she had bought the washing machine and the dish-washer.

'Wouldn't it be useful for heating up the things you've made?' she asked.

'Those,' said Marijke, 'are for cold. Now I make the risotto.'

For the next twenty-four hours, Henny kept out of the kitchen. She tried to persuade Marijke to take half an hour off to come up the street and call on Cecilia. 'No,' said Marijke, slicing pimentoes. 'I meet her tomorrow. Pay my respects.'

'You will come?' Henny said to Cecilia.

'I don't care for parties.'

'I know you're tired by evening.'

'Tired? Certainly not. I never get tired. I just get bored by meeting all these same people, again and again. I used to have to do it. I needn't, now.'

'You would give me great pleasure. And my mother will be disappointed if you don't come.'

'Very well, then.'

After Henny had gone, Cecilia contemplated going out to tidy up the remnants of the Michaelmas daisies, but switched on the TV and fell fast asleep.

It wasn't until five o'clock that Henny was able to persuade her mother to go upstairs and unpack. 'See,' said Marijke, still flushed from her efforts, 'I have brought with me a nice thing to wear.' She had bundled a frock into her suitcase, bought at the last minute in the market once she was satisfied with all the delicacies she had spent five days shopping for.

'It's lovely, Ma,' said Henny. It was. Very dark green, very plain. 'Must have cost a fortune.'

'You've forgotten the market, then,' said Marijke.

Jack came home that evening to delicious smells. 'Is this for the party?' he asked, indicating a dish of melting lamb.

'Certainly not.' Marijke had made a separate meal for her son-in-law.

At bedtime Henny felt quite able to put her arm round Jack's shoulders. She stroked the back of his head. Jack turned towards her, hands feeling and reaching.

'Just a minute,' said Henny. 'I must just go down and see that everything is turned off. My mother might have switched on the microwave by accident.'

When she got back into bed, Jack was still eager. Henny giggled. 'Darling, Ma's only across the landing. She might hear.'

'She's far too polite to listen. Anyway, we're married. It's what she'd expect us to be doing. Making babies.'

The pills were finished. For a moment, Henny was rigid with fright. Jack, sensitive to every muscle of his beloved but believing that only the proximity of her mother was inhibiting her, went sweetly and carefully until she unwound and then wound up again. The gentle result was joyful and Jack slept happily, hoping he had left a part of himself where it ought to be.

On Saturday morning Henny explained to her mother that a girl called Maxine would be coming in, to help. Marijke sniffed.

'To hand things round,' said Henny.

'I can hand my own food round.'

'Maxine needs the money.'

This, Marijke could understand. 'Where did you get this cucumber?' she asked, picking up the plastic-coated cucumber Henny had bought at the village shop. 'I can't get .it open. Where I buy they don't have to hide the vegetables.'

Henny examined the offending object. 'Oh well,' she said, wrestling unsuccessfully with the thing, 'at least no one can get AIDS from it.' Marijke did not understand the joke.

The party was to begin at 6.30. To be there in good time, Maxine went into her slot of a bedroom at five o'clock and dressed in what she considered to be a sober and suitable costume for Mrs Dormer's party. It was much the same as she had worn when waiting at Penelope's wedding party. She had to push her little brothers out of the way while she ironed her clean white shirt. She only had the same black skirt to wear, split up the back. She washed her hair, but it was still a bit colourful.

A mile away, Major Blunt was getting into his blazer. While he was settling his tight white collar, his lady wife was swigging a drop of brandy, to make herself feel younger and less out of place. It didn't seem to do much good, so she chased it with a gin and tonic and felt a little better but her husband had still not come downstairs. He was a dressy fellow and meticulous about knotting his tie. She added a little more gin, while she waited. She had taken a lot of trouble with her appearance, and spent money. Having much admired the costume Lady Lucy had worn at her daughter's wedding, she had scoured Ashden to find something a bit like it. It wasn't quite like it but it wasn't too bad, especially after one brandy and two gins.

She heard the Major coming downstairs and reapplied her lipstick. Once, she had been such a pretty girl.

'Ready?' asked the Major.

'Do I look all right?' asked Mrs Blunt. The Major straightened his tie in the hall mirror. 'Fine,' he said, not looking at her.

Mrs Phillips wore steel-grey. Dr Phillips wore his thornproof suit. Having been instructed to attend the young Dormers' party, he had fiddled about in the garden until it was time to change. But only over Mrs Phillips's dead body would they be first to arrive. Dr Phillips was overworked, and that was her word on the subject. He was made to drink a cup of tea and eat some dry biscuits before he was allowed to leave the house.

Mrs Merritt dressed to compete with her dear friend Mrs Phillips. She was fatter than Mrs Phillips but had always thought of herself as being at least better off, though goodness knew what would happen now, the way banks were going. But she could still afford Laura Ashley.

By 6.45, Mulberry Cottage was crammed to the doors when Penelope and Brian arrived. Mrs Phillips was pleased with her own timing, as she pushed through the front door side by side with Penelope. 'I hear good news of you,' she said.

Maxine handed round trays of red and white wine. She recognised Mr and the Hon. Mrs Transom, Brian's parents. Compassionately, she made for Brian and thrust a glass of wine into his hand. 'You, Mrs Transom?' she said to Penelope.

'Oh no. Just water, for me. Bottled, if you have it.'

74

Bloody nuisance, thought Maxine, running the kitchen tap. 'Aren't you going in, Mrs Brack?' she asked.

'Oh yes. I will. I must, mustn't I?'

'Yes. I think so,' said Maxine gently.

Mrs Boxendale tottered in, leaning on her ebony stick. She had gone to some trouble to look magnificent and she had succeeded. Mrs Phillips bustled over to her. 'Now, we must find you a chair. Do sit down.'

Mrs Boxendale stared. She had become mistress of this stare. It had the effect of making its recipients feel she might get her lorgnette out of her beaded handbag at any moment. It caused Mrs Phillips to laugh nervously. She had been put in her place.

Henny pushed through the crowd and was shaken hands with by Mrs Boxendale, who did not care for all this kissing on both cheeks everyone indulged in these days. 'I'm so glad you've come. I want you to meet my mother.'

To Mrs Phillips's chagrin, Marijke Brack, a complete outsider, drifted Mrs Boxendale into the perfect sitting position, in a tall, rush-seated chair with slender arms of old elm. 'I will not sit, for the moment, if you will excuse me,' said Marijke.

Mrs Boxendale bowed. She found a table placed at her elbow, upon which Marijke Brack placed a little plate of the very things to eat that Cecilia most liked. 'Glass of wine, madam?' said Maxine. She and Mrs Boxendale exchanged conspiratorial smiles. They both knew that Maxine was calling her madam in a voice loud enough to be heard by Mrs Phillips and Mrs Merritt.

'Lucy,' cried Mrs Phillips. 'Lovely to see you. I've been so busy I haven't had a moment to call.'

'Don't worry,' said Lucy, hoping that Mrs Phillips never would.

Mrs Merritt joined them. 'I'm so glad to find a moment to talk to you. We must talk about the Christmas bazaar.'

'Oh,' said Lucy, 'you and Mrs Phillips do it so well.'

'How sweet of you to say so. But I'm afraid we're going to have to fall back on you . . .'

'Not for cakes, I trust!' said Lucy. 'I can hardly compete in that department.'

75

Mrs Merritt laughed appreciatively. 'Oh no. No, we may have to come down on you to open it.'

'Don't tell me I'm all you've got?'

Mrs Merritt had the grace to look slightly embarrassed. 'We had tried,' she admitted, 'to get that actor, he's in one of those TV serials, he's just bought the old school house. His wife's an actress, too. Have you heard of them?'

'I might have done, if you could perhaps remember their names,' said Lucy, gently.

'Oh, you know, he played the doctor and she's the patient who dies. He's Doctor Something and she's the other man's wife. I don't usually watch such rubbish, but that one's a bit different.'

Lucy patted Mrs Merritt on the arm. She knew, and everyone knew, that Mrs Merritt spent her day in two ways. She either followed in the wake of Mrs Phillips or watched television. Her husband was on the verge of redundancy. She knew this from Peter. She had picked it up one evening when Peter, who usually, as breadwinner and head of the house, talked no shop at home, said unexpectedly, 'Phew. I'll tell you something. I'm very glad I set up my own partnership. Times may be hard, but at least I can't get fired, like that poor devil Merritt. Three girls and a computer, that's what banking's going to be from now on.'

'I must go and mingle. So must you.' Lucy tactfully escaped.

Major Blunt was busy hobnobbing with Brian's mother and father. Mr Transom had a soldierly look. 'Army?' enquired Major Blunt, squaring his shoulders and trying to stand as tall as Mr Transom.

'No.'

'Would have said Guards,' said Major Blunt. 'I'm ex-army myself.'

Mr Transom, who was not usually perceptive, smiled vaguely and moved away, thinking 'Pay-corps, probably.' For once in his life, he was right.

Every time Maxine passed through with her tray of glasses of wine, Mrs Blunt picked one off, some red, some white. Maxine, who was not judgmental, did wonder if nice Mrs Blunt had noticed how much she was putting away.

Mrs Boxendale was beginning to look a little tired. Mrs Phillips, far too dauntless to have seen a snub when she got it, pushed to her side. 'Any time you feel like going home, dear Mrs Boxendale, don't hesitate to ask for an arm.'

'I will have another glass of wine before I leave. Thank you, Maxine.'

'My pleasure, madam.'

'You're a marvel,' said Mrs Phillips. 'So independent. Still, watch it with the refreshments, won't you? We don't want your blood pressure shooting up, do we?'

'Don't we? I thought we did. I thought we, by which I suppose you mean you, wished to get old wrecks like me into your nursing home.'

'Where's my lady wife?' enquired Major Blunt, pulling out his pocket watch.

He did not know that Marijke, observing a green pallor upon the face of that nice fat little lady, had already escorted her up to the bathroom.

Mrs Boxendale rose. 'Jack,' she said, 'would you be so kind as to give me an arm up the street?'

Dot Blunt, having fallen into a doze on the bathroom floor, awoke and stood upright like a brave hero. She was damned if she would be sick. It took her a few minutes to remember where she was. The smartest party in Tiddingfold. The night out she'd dressed for, to please her testy husband.

She stood at the head of the stairs. Trying to descend with dignity, she missed her footing and tumbled ignominiously, all the way down.

The party, to all intents and purposes, was over.

8

On Sunday morning the Blunt household was wrapped in silence, punitive on Major Blunt's part, sick and ashamed on Dot's, until twelve minutes past ten. At that point, Major Blunt knotted his tie. 'You'd better hurry up,' he snapped.

Dot, sitting at her dressing table and grieving for her face, heard the bells. 'Church? I think I'll stay at home, if you don't mind.'

'I suppose you've forgotten what day this is? The service is at the War Memorial. That may not mean anything to you but it does to me.'

Of course! The tie; his Remembrance Service tie. Dot knew regimental ties, she wasn't a publican's daughter for nothing. This was a Gunner's tie. Years ago, she had asked him how he came to be wearing it. 'Attached,' was all he replied. She knew better than to ask any more about it.

Now, she pulled down an eyelid which took its time going up again. 'I've felt ever so ill all night. I think I've got a touch of food poisoning.'

'Food poisoning,' he snorted. 'You didn't eat any food. God knows how many glasses of wine you had. You look dreadful in that jumper and skirt. No, don't change, there isn't time. Just put on your black coat and hurry up. And a hat, for heaven's sake. Show a bit of respect. And at least it'll hide that hair.'

Dot shivered at the War Memorial. Tears were not far away; the Remembrance Service always made her want to cry anyway. The old woolly jumper rubbed unpleasantly inside the too-tight black coat. It made her feel as if her skin was on inside out. Maybe she'd got a chill coming on. Chill? Hangover, my girl, she told herself miserably.

All the Dormer clan were there, Penelope drooping against her husband and hoping to faint. Dot knew, all Tiddingfold knew, that Lady Lucy's daughter was expecting. Then she saw Henny and Jack, the handsomest couple there. For all that she had drunk too much at the party, she would take a guess that Henny had so far escaped potential motherhood. Tentatively, she smiled at Henny. Henny didn't smile back. Dot didn't realise that Henny simply didn't recognise her, in the ugly black coat and saggy, pulled-down hat. In her humbled state, she believed Henny had cut her, and she wouldn't blame her.

Cecilia Boxendale seldom allowed herself to think about Nigel. What was the good of it? His long-gone boyhood was lost in a faded mist. Like many women of her class and generation, she had had little to do with her son's upbringing. First there was Nanny, who allowed visits to the drawing-room from five o'clock until six o'clock and made it plain that cuddling, if permitted at all, was her province and not Mummy's. And then Reginald's determination to make a man of the boy, rather as though he was putting a jigsaw puzzle together without regard for the shape of its pieces. Prep school, public school. And then Nigel's sudden death in France. The one and only time Cecilia had been allowed to feel that she was her son's mother. The letter from Nigel's Commanding Officer had been written to her. Not to Reginald. For this reason, she made the pilgrimage each year to the village war memorial, her only union with her dead son.

She stood a little apart. Jack Dormer, seeing her, came over and put his arm round her. He offered his kindness in silence, for which Cecilia was grateful. She was never quite sure what her thoughts were on these annual occasions.

Jack, remembering his childhood fondness, thought how sad it was that his dear old friend had been deprived of grand-motherhood. He thought he would ask her to be a godmother to the child he and Henny would have. Well, a deputy god-mother. Godparents should be the same age as parents. But he was sure the gesture would give her pleasure.

On Monday morning, Marijke travelled back to London with Jack. He had pressed her to stay longer. What's more, he meant it. 'I'll come again,' she said, and kissed him. 'You are a good, kind man.' It was a comfort to her to know that Henny would never be left to bring up a child on her own, as she had. Not that there seemed to be any sign of a child, more was the pity. Henny needed settling. 'I go now because I want to.' And she did. The country was lovely but Marijke had long belonged to her tower block. She wanted to get back inside her own flat, which would doubtless be smothered in dust after three days' absence. And the old lady down the walkway. Had she really understood about her being away on Sunday morning? There had not been a Sunday morning in years upon which Marijke had not taken her a dinner. There were no meals on wheels on Sundays.

She sat looking out of the train window. Jack was reading the papers he had taken out of his briefcase. The fecklessness of her own husband had failed to shake Marijke's inborn acceptance of the rule that said male requirements transcended all. If a man was silent, you were silent. If he spoke, you answered.

At Sevenoaks, Jack looked up from his document and said, 'Thank you so much for coming to help with the party. You made it, you know.'

'I told Henny to make noodles tonight, with the meatballs. There were some left.'

'I'm in luck, then. Everyone was eating so much. My mother said it was the first time she'd ever been to a party like it. I expect you've started a new fashion. You could make a fortune as a caterer, in Tiddingfold.'

Marijke was very pleased indeed. Jack's words wiped out a nasty little exchange she had heard between Mrs Merritt and Mrs Phillips:

'My dear, what on *earth* is this?'

'Seems to be some sort of stew. Odd thing to have at a drinks party. Still, I suppose we must expect changes, these days. New people.'

'The mother's Hungarian or something, isn't she? Eugh, it's full of garlic.'

'Better see Cecilia doesn't have any.'

Marijke's English was not subtle. But she knew enough to recognise Mrs Phillips's familiarity, using Mrs Boxendale's

Christian name behind her back. She was sure that woman no more addressed Mrs Boxendale as Cecilia to her face than did that other woman, Mrs Merritt. There was something about Mrs Phillips that Marijke didn't trust.

'She shouldn't really come out at night,' Marikje had heard Mrs Merritt say, following Mrs Phillips's lead as usual. 'Let's hope your poor husband isn't called out tomorrow.'

Mrs Phillips rewarded her with a laugh and a condescending glance round the room. 'It's rather like *EastEnders*, isn't it?'

At Charing Cross, Jack wanted to put Marijke into a taxi. Marijke wanted no such thing. But she followed him out of the station obediently. There was a long queue at the taxi rank. 'Please, do not wait,' said Marijke. It took her quite a time to get rid of Jack, after which she found her own way home. She got lost three times, on the underground.

Jack, at last persuaded by Marijke that she could manage, rushed out into the Strand and grabbed a taxi. He could have got to the office quicker on foot.

There was no way into his own office except past Glenda's desk. Glenda had managed to turn a small section of corridor into a cross between an ante-room and a bower. She had surrounded herself with pots of expensive indoor growths, the sort that look a bit sinister, if you see it that way. Kevin Preston-Jackson obviously didn't. He was sitting on the edge of Glenda's desk, swinging a long leg.

'I'll be with you in a moment.' Jack pulled off his coat.

Kevin followed him slowly, with all the calm of a man who has got in early and already dismissed a few problems. 'Train trouble?' he enquired, as Jack's coat fell off the bentwood stand. 'You need a coffee. I was just going to have one myself.' He called through the door 'Glenda, get us some coffee, there's a sweetheart.' Having gained the advantage, he remained standing. He still had a way to go. In any case, only a fool would sit in one of the two low, squashy chairs on the recipient side of Jack's desk, with the light from the window behind Jack's seat shining straight into his face.

Jack began to go through the papers before him. 'The soap report's there,' said Kevin, pointing helpfully. 'I got Glenda to type it up on Friday evening.'

'Good. Thank you Kevin. Well done. I'll just take it up to the MD.'

'He was looking for it, earlier. He came in at 9.30. I told him I was sure you'd bring it up as soon as you got here.'

'Thank you, Kevin.' Jack took a sip of his coffee. It had milk and sugar in it. He always took his coffee black, no sugar. Glenda knew that perfectly well. Still, he reflected, it really was not the business of a highly paid, efficient secretary to do the job of coffee-lady.

'You haven't drunk your coffee,' said Kevin solicitously. His cup was just as he liked it.

Major and Mrs Blunt had spent the Sunday afternoon after the Remembrance Service in renewed, and grimmer, silence. Dot had tried to make up for her misdemeanours with roast lamb. Unfortunately, she had never got the hang of the time-clock on the oven. By two o'clock she could have shaved off some edible portions from the outside but she knew better than to try. The inside would be raw, and no good telling her all-British husband the French liked it that way. They sat down at three.

Major Blunt had two pink gins. Dot, hoping he would notice, refrained from having anything at all in the alcoholic line. She stuck to her guns all day, in spite of gloom amounting to panic throughout the long afternoon.

She found herself alone at last, on Monday morning. There was a meeting of the British Legion in Ashden and Major Blunt drove off to make his point about a better organised, more soldierly appearance at next year's memorial services.

What Dot really wanted to do was to go back to bed and reread *Rebecca*. It always made her feel slim again, every time she reacquainted herself with the second Mrs de Winter. But she was made of sterner stuff than she gave herself credit for.

She washed her face. She combed her hair. She looked into the mirror and decided she'd stop messing about with the Lady Clairol. She took the scissors and clipped off a few of the over-dyed ends. Then she decided what to wear. There was a twin-set, a so far unused present from her grown-up daughter. Marie was married to an insurance broker. The twin-set was mauve, but quite nice, really. With a tweed skirt and a pair of shoes she could manage to walk in, Dot Blunt set out. She would never be able to face young Mrs Dormer again if she didn't do it now.

Braced by her walk, and resolute, she rang Henny's front door bell. She rang it twice. It was a bell ringing in an empty house. All effort crumbling, cast down, she began to walk away. Turning back, she saw Mrs Phillips outside the village shop. To cover her confusion, she went in the other direction. The other direction took her past Mrs Boxendale's house.

As luck would have it, Henny was glancing out of Mrs Boxendale's front window when she saw Mrs Blunt. 'Do you mind if I ask her in?' Henny asked Cecilia.

There was no getting away. Dot found herself seated. 'We were just talking about the party,' said Mrs Boxendale. 'The best party for years, in Tiddingfold. I was congratulating Henny.'

'And doing me a power of good,' said Henny. 'I was scared to death. I didn't know how it would go.'

'I didn't help, did I?' said Dot.

'What *do* you mean?'

That *would* be what Mrs Boxendale would say, a lady to her fingertips. 'I mean I didn't behave very well,' said Dot, resolutely. In the ensuing silence, she added, 'I drank too much.'

'We all do. It's one's only comfort. Henny dear, get Mrs Blunt a glass of sherry, will you?'

9

Christmas was coming. The head-teacher of Tiddingfold primary school, who was approaching retirement and glad of it, decided to go for a Nativity play and be damned. As far as the children were concerned, it made not a hoot of difference whether they were Joseph and Mary or Muslims or Hindus, as long as they could put on coloured head-dresses and wave to their mums and dads in the audience.

Mrs Phillips and Mrs Merritt got the Christmas bazaar going. Mrs Phillips very generously sacrificed Alma's three hours a week and cleaned her own bathroom. Alma thoroughly enjoyed being promoted to putting the village hall to rights for this important public occasion. It didn't come home to her until too late that Mrs Phillips had given of her services free. Rising in society had cost Alma £3.50 an hour.

Heraclitus had settled into his box of leaves and hay. He woke from a pleasant drowse to find his beak being opened and filled with cod-liver oil. Lucy stroked his neck and he went peacefully to sleep.

Cecilia Boxendale received a telephone call from her daughter Betty.

Betty Boxendale telephoned her mother at six o'clock on a Thursday evening. She was careful about the bills. It always irritated her when her mother answered the telephone and then made her wait while she turned off the television and then usually dropped the receiver while re-seating herself. But this evening the telephone went on ringing ten times before it was picked up.

'Were you in bed?' asked Betty. Mrs Boxendale, these days, seldom went to bed before midnight. It was the only way she could sleep at all.

'Who is it?'

'It's me.'

'Who's me?' Cecilia knew her daughter's voice perfectly well.

'Me. Betty.' Unable to recognise perversity, Betty decided her mother was either getting deaf or gaga. 'How are you?' she enunciated.

'There's no need to bellow. I'm perfectly well, thank you. And how are you?'

'I was just thinking, I haven't seen you for a long time.'

'No. Well, you know where I live.' Hearing herself sound tart, Cecilia added in a kinder voice, 'You must come down, some time.'

'I'd like to. I was thinking of Christmas, actually.'

'Oh. It'll be rather dull for you.'

'Bobby's going away.'

'I see. And if your friend is going away – ' which was no doubt why Betty had suddenly decided to spend Christmas with her aged mother – 'what is going to happen to all your dogs?'

'Bobby's going to take hers with her. You won't mind if I bring Jasper?'

'Is he very large?'

'Not very. Quite small, for a lab, really. And Jody.'

'*Two*?'

'Jody's Jasper's wife. They don't like to be separated.'

'How sweet.'

Taking despondent sarcasm for assent, Betty, assuring her mother how much they were all looking forward to seeing her, rang off.

Lucy, coming in the day after this, could see at once that Cecilia was agitated. She hadn't long to wait to uncover the cause.

'It's about Christmas, Lucy. I'm rather worried.'

'You're spending Christmas Day with us, I hope?'

'That's the trouble. Betty has said she's coming to stay.'

'That's all right. She'll come too, surely?'

'Well, at least that's one day off my mind.' Mending her manners, Cecilia added, 'I mean, thank you so much. I'm sorry,

Lucy, I'm in a bit of a bother. She wants to stay for a week and she's bringing two dogs.'

'Oh dear. I'd say put her in a bed and breakfast but I can't think of anywhere they'd take the dogs, even if there was any such thing round here as a b. & b. that stayed open over Christmas. At least perhaps you'll let me help you get her room ready.'

'Maxine's very willing. She's such a good child. But thank you, I would feel happier if you could spare time to give her a hand.'

'Of course I will. I still think it's far too much for you. But never mind, it can't be helped now and we'll muddle along somehow.'

For a while, Cecilia felt better. But then Mrs Phillips, getting word of the coming event, steamed in. 'What's this I hear, my dear?'

'I don't know, I'm afraid. But I'm sure you'll tell me.'

'About Betty. I hear she's coming to stay for the Christmas holidays. It'll all round the village. They say she's bringing a pack of hounds.'

'My daughter is not a hunting woman. She is simply bringing two dogs. Two small dogs.'

'Now, you know I never interfere. But it's far too much for you. Far too much. We'll have your blood pressure up. At your age, it could be positively dangerous.'

'You mean, I'll have a stroke? If I do, I promise you I'll make sure to die of it. You're not getting me into the Elms yet, my dear Mrs Phillips.'

Cecilia having triumphantly showed Mrs Phillips to the door, went straight to the telephone and rang Henny to come round for a glass of sherry.

'I was just starting to put up some decorations.'

'Oh dear, I've interrupted.'

'You couldn't have chosen a better moment. I'll be right round.'

At two o'clock the day before Christmas Eve, Betty arrived. Typical Betty, no idea how difficult it is for a hostess to think what to do when it isn't time for drinks or a meal. Still, Cecilia chided herself, the poor girl *is* my daughter. 'Come in, come in,' she said.

The dogs were already in. If Jasper was a small labrador, heaven knew what a large one must be like. Jody, though neither so long or so tall as Jasper, was grossly overweight. Still, one good thing: it was soon clear that they weren't going to have to sit awkwardly and try to make conversation. Betty was busy as could be. First of all, the dogs had to be let out. Fortunately, Cecilia didn't notice that Jasper managed to lift his leg *before* getting to the garden. Both dogs managed to get muddy and Betty had to rush out to her car for the doggie-towels, while the animals helpfully dried themselves on the hall carpet.

Soon a noxious smell came from the kitchen. 'Don't worry, I'm just cooking their melts. No need to come, I've found a saucepan. Don't move.'

Having no desire to find out what melts were, Cecilia decided to obey. No doubt Betty was using that nice new saucepan Henny had given her. But never mind. You don't need a saucepan for salt biscuits and cream cheese.

Later on, Lucy came in. She had guessed that Betty would arrive in time to make it a long afternoon for Cecilia.

'You know you're coming to us for Christmas Day? You and your mother,' she said.

'Thank you, how nice,' said Betty. 'The dogs will be all right here. It's always difficult to leave one, alone. But the two of them are fine together.' Lucy was glad to hear it.

'Your mother's freezer section is full of goodies,' she said. 'You needn't worry about her having to cook. And we're having a huge turkey, so there'll be some cold for you on Boxing Day.' Betty was busy examining the ears of the fat dog. 'I'm doing a large ham as well. That will be nice cold, too,' yelled Lucy.

'Actually,' said Betty. 'I'm a vegetarian.'

'Why didn't you tell me?' asked Cecilia.

'I didn't want to be a bother.'

Lucy, who had herself shopped for the frozen chilli con carne, chicken *à la* king and sliced lamb in gravy she had been sure Betty would enjoy, wished Betty was young enough to be smacked. 'Never mind,' she smiled. 'The shop's still open. I believe they have vegetable lasagnes and things like that. There's just time for you to go and buy some.'

On the way home, she called in on Henny.

'Let her eat sprouts,' was Henny's opinion.

'I wish your mother was coming,' said Lucy.

'Can't budge her. The landing-gang can't have Christmas without Ma.'

'Haven't got much selection,' said Betty, returning from the village shop. 'We always get ours at Tesco's. Bobby cooks, sometimes. We had a judge to dinner the other week. She turned out a jolly nice thing, soya and prune stew.'

'A judge?' enquired Cecilia. 'High Court or Circuit?'

'No. King Charles.'

'King Charles? I don't think I've heard of that sort of judge. Is it a sort of sheriff?'

'No. Spaniels.'

Maxine was preparing for Christmas Day more happily than ever before. She couldn't get over the lovely present Mrs Boxendale had given her. Those dogs, though. The big one, Jasper, kept sticking his nose up her skirt. And that nice saucepan, crusted. She gave it a good scrub. 'Bedroom looks nice, Lady Lucy,' she said. One day, she'd have a guest-room with flowers in, like Lady Lucy had done. Fancy, just a bit of that forsythia and who would have thought there'd be marigolds still out, in the garden. And in a cup. You learn something every day.

On the way home, she opened the envelope Mrs Boxendale had put into her hand. She thought, 'A card. Nice of her.' It was £20. Maxine had never had that much money in her hand before. It was soon spent. A bottle of scent for Mum, toys for her little brothers. For all her dad got on her nerves, she couldn't leave him out. Serve him right if I got him a Black and Decker, she thought. But she couldn't afford that, so she bought him a Do-It-Yourself book.

On Christmas Eve, Mrs Phillips took Betty to see the Nativity play at the school. 'Don't expect too much, my dear. I don't suppose Tiddingfold standards are up to yours.'

'I'm sure I shall enjoy it very much,' said Betty, flattered.

Mrs Phillips nodded graciously about her as she led Betty into the school. 'One must support these things. So many of the village people don't seem to take the slightest interest in their own community. They just expect to have everything done for them, these days,' she said, quite loudly enough to offend anyone within hearing distance.

Throughout the performance, Mrs Phillips asked Betty's opinion and was given it. It was a pity the singing hadn't been better rehearsed and really, the first thing one had to do with small children was to teach them to speak up. Sour looks from behind, in front and beside them would have made it plain to more sensitive recipients that the ability to speak up was not lacking in either Betty Boxendale or Mrs Phillips. Mrs Merritt, ousted from where she had expected to sit, next to her dear friend Mrs Phillips, was perched uncomfortably at the end of a lesser row at the back, resolutely remaining loyal and pretending she was only sitting here because she was so busy she'd arrived late.

Mrs Phillips escorted her new firm friend home and was taken in for coffee. Mrs Boxendale went to bed.

Major and Mrs Blunt's daughter spent Christmas Day with them. Mrs Blunt remembered to wear the twin-set. Marie's husband gave Major Blunt advice about insurance. Their two children watched the television. Dot made a pretty table, put the turkey in the oven and felt fortunate to be able to spend the morning in the kitchen, where she could sip a drink unseen. She had made stuffing for both ends of the turkey. In the old days, at the pub, her mum had been renowned for her cooking. Dot wasn't very confident, so she had got recipes out of *Woman's Own*. The back end of the turkey was filled with chestnuts, lemon juice and chopped bacon. The front had sausage meat, breadcrumbs, nuts and mustard. Emma and Alison laid both stuffings, without even tasting them, on the side of their plates, and then picked over their portions of turkey with a fastidious-ness that made Dot long to slap them and ask how they'd like to be in Bosnia. They really depressed her. She could remember things she hadn't liked to eat when she was little and she would have loved to sympathise. But the sorrow of it was, she didn't much like them. Marie was expecting another child. A boy. The tests had said so.

Christmas Day at Alexandra Lodge went off rather well, on the whole. Peter Dormer listened kindly to Betty, who talked of dogs. He remembered a long-ago fox-terrier, briefly a member of the household of his youth until it met a premature end under the wheels of a passing car. 'I'll get you to advise me. Penelope's expecting, you know. I'll get a puppy for the baby.'

Betty gave him a long dissertation on not getting the puppy first, jealousy *et seq.*, choice of puppy, age of child and so on. Her words flowed pleasantly in and out of Peter's ears as he carved the turkey. Betty, believing herself to be interesting, ate a large portion of turkey without even noticing.

Jack thought Henny had never looked prettier. He liked her a little plumper; not that she should put on any more weight, yet. In the middle of Christmas pudding and port, he was overwhelmed with a desire to get her home and into bed. Luckily, Mrs Boxendale was looking tired. As soon as possible after coffee, he offered to take her and Betty home.

On Cecilia's doorstep, Henny refused the invitation to come in. Cecilia, she could see, had had enough for one day. And Betty could attend to her dogs quite well on her own.

Cecilia, entering ahead of Betty, was the first to discover the reason for Jody's apparent obesity. Jasper was dashing about, wringing his paws. Under the hall table lay Jody. The hall carpet was smothered in newborn puppies.

'Oh dear,' said Betty, 'she wasn't due to whelp for over a week. I hope she's all right.'

Mrs Boxendale gripped the banisters and made her way upstairs. Looking back, she saw her daughter crawling on hands and knees around the hall, like an ungainly swimmer in a school of jellyfish. This was going to be one day upon which she was glad to go to bed early.

10

On Boxing Day, all Tiddingfold assembled for the Meet. Tiddingfold was proud, in these degenerate days, of its traditions. People who never saw each other from one year's end to the next gathered in the most friendly manner, on the green. The Woodcutter's Arms debouched on the green and Boxing Day was a good day for its landlord. Well, manager. He was twenty-eight and newly shifted into this godforsaken hole, having failed to make his previous pub, or outlet, as the brewers called it, pay.

Dot Blunt rather liked this sort of thing. She could slip into the pub and commiserate with the manager's wife, like an elder statesman. Major Blunt, in his element, turned out attired for the occasion in cavalry twill. Even Penelope, that erstwhile rider to gymkhanas, tottered along with Brian in tow.

Peter Dormer enjoyed it, too. Never having had the opportunity of learning to ride himself, he had gained particular satisfaction from seeing his beautifully turned out daughter on these annual occasions, astride the pony whose mane he had plaited himself. 'Marvellous seat, though I say it myself,' he would say knowingly. And Penelope had had a marvellous seat, for as long as the pony stood still and there were plenty of people watching her. And now his good little girl was well on the way to providing the family with its next pony-club candidate.

Mrs Phillips greeted Betty as an old friend. 'You a hunting woman?' enquired Betty.

Mrs Phillips laughed. 'You can hear my Irish accent, can't you? But no, I'm more medical. Trained in Dublin. Dublin is a great city for medical training. Not that I'm a doctor, don't think that. Just a nurse. That's how I met my husband.'

'I often used to wish I'd gone in for nursing. So worthwhile. But Father wouldn't hear of it.' Reginald Boxendale had had some pretty salacious notions of nurses, not, perhaps, totally understood by his innocent daughter. Even so, her recollections of what Father had had to say on the subject caused Betty to look apologetically at Mrs Phillips and add, 'I think it was just that he didn't want me to leave home.'

'Ah,' said Mrs Phillips, sagely, 'the daughter at home. We see a lot of that. Caring for elderly parents.'

'But Tiddingfold's such a wonderful place,' said Betty. 'My mother has so many friends.'

'She has, indeed.' For a moment, Mrs Phillips could see she had lost Betty Boxendale's attention. Betty was pulling a hound out of the Woodcutter's Arms' dustbin and hauling something out of its mouth.

'Chicken bones. Typical. They don't think. If that goes through the animal, its intestine could be split in half.'

'Are you going to follow?' asked Mrs Phillips.

'Can't. Must get back. Jody had her puppies yesterday. And we're lunching with Henny and Jack.'

'Your mother as well? Are you sure that's wise? Going out today as well as yesterday.'

'You try and stop her!' laughed Betty. 'Anyway, she's as tough as old boots.'

'I wouldn't be so sure.' Mrs Phillips managed to slip a note of veiled doom into her voice.

'She's not ill, is she?' To Betty people were ill or perfectly well.

'Oh dear no, not as such. She's wonderful, for her age. But there are . . . things.'

'What things?'

'Nothing unusual. I keep an eye on her as best I can.'

'You're very good. Very kind.'

Mrs Phillips waved the praise aside. 'Don't think of it. Still, I'm glad to have a little talk with you. Really, you see, your mother shouldn't be living alone.'

'Are you saying I ought to come and live with her?' Betty's face was nakedly aghast, as Mrs Phillips had intended it should be.

'Oh dear no. I don't approve of that at all. That's just what I was trying to explain to you. I've seen far too many daughters' lives ruined that way. So sad, when it never really works in any case. The worst thing possible.'

'Then what ought I to do?'

Mrs Phillips took the plunge. 'I can help you, there. There's a very good nursing home, the Elms.'

'But she doesn't need nursing, surely?'

'Nursing home's just a name. It's residential, with nursing available. I'm on the board, you see – ' she didn't add that she owned the place – 'so I have a little influence. I could get her in.'

While Betty was once again thanking Mrs Phillips for her kindness and concern, Cecilia was in her kitchen, surveying a large cardboard box full of blind but vocal puppies. Jody, hideously milky, was whining at the back door to get out to Jasper. 'It's all right for him, isn't it?' said Cecilia, letting the boring mother labrador out and thinking thank goodness she'd soon be going to Henny's house for lunch.

Betty panted in and dragged Jody back from the garden. Having stuffed her into the box of puppies, she boiled up milk and water and mixed it with something smelly from a carton. Recoiling, Cecilia said 'Don't you think you ought to change? Just a skirt, or even a clean pair of trousers. We're due at Henny and Jack's in ten minutes.'

'Do you think you ought to go, Mother?'

'I most certainly do.' Cecilia had taken some trouble to dress herself quite splendidly in a grey costume and a pink blouse carefully ironed by Maxine.

'As long as you're sure it isn't too much for you?' Betty peered at her mother, searching for the signs of frailty Mrs Phillips had managed to suggest.

'I really don't think so.' What would be too much for her would be to remain within olfactory distance of all this squirming livestock. She took her ebony stick and walked pointedly towards the front door.

Lunch was the same assembly as yesterday. During it, Peter Dormer heard at length about Jody's puppies and what a pity it was that it was too soon for Penelope's future baby to have one, but there would be plenty more to come.

There were plenty of delicious salads. Henny had gone to considerable trouble. Her culinary skills had come on but, even so, she felt safer with a cold collation and an elegantly prepared table. She had bought a sort of kitchen-lectern, upon which she propped that nice Delia Smith who put her instructions in words a person could understand. Even so, she had been up since dawn, anxious about the exact minute when dressing should be added to green salad, how soon she could butter the bread and had the mayonnaise separated and, if so, what the hell was she going to do about it?

Cecilia was not keen on salad but was too polite not to finish up the over-filled plate Betty, herself munching enthusiastically, put before her. Betty, she noted, had *not* changed her clothes. There was puppy-sick on her trousers. Her daughter, Cecilia noted, had a unique talent for uniting meekness with quite considerable aggressiveness: you must-take-me-as-you-find-me, this-is-the-way-I-am. A few glasses of champagne, for Jack was as generous as his father with the wine, took away the taste of salad and it all floated down as though her digestive tract was forty years younger.

'Well done, Henny,' said Peter Dormer genially. He was no keener on salads than Cecilia but he had decided to encourage his daughter-in-law. 'Welcome to the family.'

'Oh,' said Henny. 'Thank you.'

'And a family we are, are we not? A growing family now. May, for you, darling,' he looked at Penelope, who was eating salad. Henny was glad she had at least produced the right vitamins and minerals for the expectant mother.

'May the fifteenth,' said Penelope importantly.

Lucy smiled. 'Darling, first babies are often late. I'd tell people May twenty something and then they won't keep ringing you up to ask if it has arrived yet.'

'Oh no. You see, Mummy, it's different from your day. Once the date is established we just go in, and if the baby's head is engaged, you are monitored. We work as a team to avoid foetal distress and the baby's bowels are so important and – '

'Yes dear.' Lucy tried not to heave.

Peter, going quite the wrong route in changing the subject, said, 'Well, now, Henny. What about you?'

'I squeezed some melon juice for you, Penelope,' said Henny desperately. 'Jack darling, did you see that Penelope had the melon juice?'

Jack was talking to Mrs Boxendale and didn't hear her.

Penelope, shrewdly picking up her sister-in-law's evasiveness, chipped in with her own idea of being helpful. 'Never mind, Henny. When you've been on the pill for years and years, I believe it takes quite a long time to get over it. Not that I know, myself.' She threw her husband a friendlier glance than he ever got at home and continued, 'No, not that I'd know myself, I married so young. But it's been so helpful, classes and all that, you know. For some women, it takes ages. But you needn't worry, there's so much that can be done. There's a fertility clinic at the hospital. You could go there. They're really nice. Their watchword is that infertility is not a failure.' She concluded her dissertation by enclosing her stomach between both hands and looking down upon it with satisfaction.

Henny was assailed by an almost hysterical desire to see the back of the lot of them. She had settled in so well. She loved her mother-in-law, she liked Cecilia. She very much liked Cecilia's sturdy little helper, Maxine. And Mrs Blunt. And for Jack's sake, she was willing to welcome a child if it came her way. But for herself, she was not sure. It would, she supposed, be a pity if the next few years brought no children. But the next few years would be time enough.

'This ham and nut salad is particularly good,' said Lucy, looking with compassion at Henny. When at last the lunch party came to an end, she hung back and put her arms round her daughter-in-law. 'Babies are so final, aren't they?' she whispered. She wasn't sure whether Henny heard her words or not.

The ham and nut salad, good or not, was the undoing of Cecilia. In the middle of the night she awoke, racked with indigestion. She was sure there were some indigestion tablets in the bathroom cabinet. There were, but the open box had been untouched for so long that the tablets had steamed themselves into an unmanageable lump. She took a drink of water and went back to bed.

In the morning, Betty took a cup of tea up to her mother. She had been up bright and early, prodding puppies, turning them upside down and examining their umbilical cords.

Mrs Boxendale groaned. She was not keen on early morning activity. But she could see this was kindly meant. She took a mouthful of over-milked tea and winced, putting her hand to her chest. Betty decided she was witnessing a heart attack, rushed to the telephone and called Mrs Phillips, who hastened to the scene.

To give Mrs Phillips her due, she knew and admitted indigestion when she saw it. 'You were right to send for me, though,' she told Betty comfortingly. 'It could have been a warning. Keep her on Complan and Lucozade for a couple of days. I'll get my husband to come as soon as he can.'

'I ought to be going, the day after tomorrow. Do you think I should?'

'Of course you should. You can leave all this to me. Give me your telephone number and I'll get in touch if necessary.'

'You are so kind,' said Betty.

On New Year's Day, the wind went round into the north and by afternoon the first snowflakes were falling. Big, irresolute star shapes at first, but very soon freezing beads that meant business. By nightfall it was lying. Overnight, Tiddingfold turned into a belated Christmas card.

Mrs Phillips had to pay the price for her pre-Christmas donation of Alma's services to the bazaar. Short-changed on that deal, Alma put her charges up to £3.75 an hour. In the confined bottom of winter, Mrs Phillips was driven mad by unpolished taps, and goodness knew, she could only do so much herself. She had to pay up. Furthermore Alma, who had hitherto gone about her business on a bicycle, now liked to be collected by car and driven home.

Maxine was thankful that school hadn't yet opened. She went to Mrs Boxendale every day. It was she who brought in the logs that stoked the sitting-room fire before which Mrs Boxendale made her place her wet shoes and stockings. Maxine had no boots. Mrs Boxendale made a foray into her cupboard and came out with an old pair of Morlands. 'They're not smart, dear child. Don't be offended.' Maxine wasn't, in the least.

At this time, Henny saw very little of Jack. The obviously sensible thing for him to do was to stay in London during this appalling weather. He was comfortable and warm, in a hotel room paid for by the firm. Henny had suggested that he use the flat in Covent Garden but immediately realised that it was empty and cold.

She was thankful that Jody's puppies were too young to leave their mother. Jack, anxious about leaving her alone at nights, had suggested a labrador, as companion and protector. Henny felt it a mercy that one week old was on the young side for a guard dog. An even greater mercy was that the snow refrained from setting in until after Betty had departed, her car groaning under the weight of Jasper and Jody's enlarged family and their appurtenances.

But set in it did. It snowed for three weeks. Lucy spaded out the driveway of Alexandra Lodge. For two days, Peter had worked from home, by telephone. Lucy, who for years had welcomed her husband's evening return in time for dinner, had her first experience of the loss of the middle of the day as her own private few hours. Luckily, hard times or no, the rural council salted the roads and Lucy's middays regained the status of for better, for worse but not for lunch.

Most days, Henny went in to see Cecilia. Cecilia's old-fashioned manners were comfortable. Cecilia would not dream of asking so impertinent a question as to whether one was pregnant. Not that Cecilia was less than *au fait* with current practices. Apart from anything else, she got idler and idler about switching off her television set, as a result of which, waking or dozing, she knew what was going on in the world which had moved so fast forward from the more secretive mores of her own young days. She didn't watch *Neighbours* and good old *Coronation Street* for nothing. It was all go in Cecilia's sitting-room. So she knew quite well the meaning of the officious advice Penelope had given Henny. 'At her own table,' she muttered disgustedly. She was sorry for Lucy, who was clearly embarrassed by the episode. She would never have mentioned it to her. But Lucy herself brought it up.

'I really must have a word with that daughter of mine.'

'I expect she meant well,' said Cecilia.

Lucy knew what *that* meant. 'The thing is, though,' she went on, 'I happen to know that Henny has come off the pill. So I'm assuming that she does want a baby.'

'I wouldn't worry about it. My own opinion is that she'd make the best of it if it happened. But it's no be-all and end-all to her.' At that moment Henny appeared and the subject was dropped.

Sometimes Henny found Dot Blunt with Cecilia. Major Blunt, it seemed, had a touch of bronchitis. Dot would leave his lunch ready and plodded along to Cecilia's house. She had a pair of wellies. 'Don't I look comical?' she would say, arranging her frivolous skirt once the wellies were pulled off in the hall.

'I like snow,' said Cecilia.

'So do I,' said Maxine. 'I'd like to make a snowman. Did you see that video? *The Snowman*, it's called.'

'Have you never made a snowman, Maxine?' asked Mrs Boxendale.

'Not myself, no.'

'Let's make one.'

'You're on. We'll do it tomorrow.' Maxine didn't want Mrs Boxendale to go outdoors in all this cold. 'I'll just Hoover round.'

'Does it need it? I expect it does. Dog-hairs. Funny, Alma hasn't been.'

'Can't get here, in all this. It's ever so slippery out.' Maxine knew full well that Alma had dropped Mrs Boxendale; £3.75 an hour and picked up and taken home, with that Mrs Phillips. Maxine plugged in the vacuum cleaner with a fierce hand. Mrs Phillips could afford that sort of money, her and her blooming Elms. 'It's all right,' she called over her shoulder, 'I won't bump the ornaments. I'll be ever so careful.'

She didn't leave until she was sure Mrs Boxendale had nodded off to sleep. Busy morning, she'd had. That nice Mrs Blunt had come in. 'Maxine,' she'd said, 'just pop this in the kitchen, will you?' 'This' was a bowl of soup. 'I tried to make it like my mother used to. Don't say it was me. I wouldn't like to give offence.' She couldn't half put away the sherry! Henny had been in, too. No sherry for her, she said she was dieting.

Henny was spending that snowy afternoon thinking, in her empty house. She screwed some cup-hooks on to the edge of the kitchen shelf. She didn't do it very well. She ached for a cigarette. She switched on the TV and watched some ads, every one of which she could have done better herself. There was no need to make dinner; Jack wouldn't be back from London. WTS, when weather dramas of this magnitude occurred, picked up the tab for pretty good hotel accommodation, so he would be perfectly comfortable and well fed.

She made herself a pot of tea. No biscuits, she was determined to knock off the pounds. No booze. The female population of Tiddingfold was afloat on a sea of sherry and gin. Even Lucy, except when she was driving. A wife in her position couldn't afford to lose her licence.

Cecilia awoke. The moon shone so brilliantly across her garden that she thought it was daylight. She was wide awake. Her house was gloriously empty. No puppies in the kitchen, no melts stewing on the stove, no Betty, no Mrs Phillips. The moonlight, coming through the window showed her an immaculately clean carpet. Maxine had done that. Nice Maxine. Maxine wanted to make a snowman.

Cecilia went through her quiet house to the back door. She opened it. The snow was as thick as an eiderdown. Laughing, strong, she began to gather up handfuls and pack them together. She began the snowman.

11

Cecilia lay all night in the snow. It felt lovely. Lovely, and warm. Once, she stood up and paddled in it. Like the sea at Frinton. Long ago, with Nanny. Nannies went to Frinton. Haven't got a nanny, now. Have. Maxine.

She was right. It was Maxine who discovered her in the morning. It was Maxine who dragged her indoors. She bent over to catch a hoarse whisper: 'Don't tell Mrs Phillips.'

'Don't you worry, let's get you in.' To herself Maxine said, 'Don't care if they put me in prison for it. Oh dear, she's wet herself. Never mind, I got clean nighties for her.'

Only when she had established Mrs Boxendale, clean and tidy, in her bed, did Maxine go for help. Maxine went and got Henny. 'She's breathing funny.'

'Do you think we ought to get Dr Phillips?' asked Henny.

'What, and get her and all? Mrs Phillips?'

'We can't do this alone. She's gasping.'

'I've sat her up. But you're right.' Maxine choked back tears. 'It'll be hospital, I suppose.'

There was nothing for it, and they both knew it, but to get Dr Phillips. 'Don't tell him about last night,' whispered Maxine.

'Are you sure we shouldn't?' asked Henny anxiously.

'Any fool can see she's got pneumonia, even him,' said Maxine reasonably. 'And if *she* gets to hear she was wandering round the garden all night, she'll be waiting at the hospital gates to nobble her when she comes out. Say she's barmy, she will. Silly cow.' Maxine alleviated her terror by allowing herself to slag off Mrs Phillips.

As it turned out, Dr Phillips, seeing his patient in her bed, simply diagnosed pneumonia, asked no questions and called the ambulance. Henny and Maxine watched as their friend was carried out, strapped into something a cross between a stretcher and a garden chair, one of her slippers tumbling into the gutter. The ambulance men were kind. They gave oxygen. 'Your gran?' said one of them to Maxine.

'No,' said Maxine with dignity, 'I am her lady's maid.' Turning back into the house with Henny, she added, 'That made them think. Wherever did I get it from?'

'Sheer inspiration,' said Henny. 'I'd have hired you for creativity. When I worked.'

Lucy drove Henny and Maxine to the hospital to see Cecilia. Maxine was worried. She wouldn't wonder if Mrs Boxendale believed she'd shopped her. But far from it. Cecilia was sitting up and taking notice. 'Look at this,' she said, indicating a needle in her wrist attached to a tube attached to a stand. 'See this coat-hanger thing? And that plastic bag. Full of goodness knows what, I asked the nurse and she said glucose to get my strength back. Marvellous, isn't it? I'll be home in no time.'

'Two weeks, at least,' said Sister in answer to Lucy's enquiries. 'She was almost one leg in heaven when they brought her in. But she's a trier. Tell me something, what is The Elms? When she was delirious she kept on about it. Was she at a school called The Elms, or something like that? She talked about hockey. And a bicycle.'

Lucy, Henny and Maxine were gathered together at Sister's desk. They gave each other looks which said, Let's not go into that. If Sister had not heard of The Elms, least said, soonest mended. 'Oh well,' said Lucy, 'I know she had a bicycle when she was a girl. And she played hockey. So she's getting on quite well, you think? We were wondering whether we should send for the daughter, her next of kin.'

'She'd like a visit, no doubt, if she's fond of the daughter. But she's not going to die this time, if that's what you're asking.' Sister looked politely but pointedly past the shoulders of Lucy, Henny and Maxine. Other people, they realised, were dying. They returned to Cecilia, found she had gone to sleep, and left.

The snow was not yet gone. Jack was still stuck in London. Henny wanted to tell him that she had been to see his old friend Mrs Boxendale. She put in a call to his office. She had a direct line to the telephone on his desk.

After six rings she was almost putting the phone down when it was answered by a voice that was not Jack's.

'Kevin Preston-Jackson.'

'Who?' asked Henny, taken aback.

'Kevin Preston-Jackson.'

'I wanted Jack Dormer.'

'He's not here, I'm afraid.' Henny heard him call loudly 'Glenda, is Jack back from lunch yet? No? Sorry. Do you want to leave a message?'

'No thank you. I'll call again.' Hell-fire, so *that* was Jack's new assistant – that snake Kevin Preston-Jackson.

School had reopened. Maxine was obliged to waste her time by attending. She could already read and write perfectly well, thank you, and what more did she need? GCSEs? Any fool could get GCSEs, and then what? No jobs. Some of her schoolfellows were passing the Easter term by planning charitable efforts. Sponsored walks, to raise money for old folks. Huh, thought Maxine, I've got better things to do than bother Henny and Lady Lucy for 40p a mile, wasting my time walking round the churchyard. I walk anyway; I walk up to Mrs Boxendale's.

'Where's Maxine?' asked Cecilia, recognising Lucy and Henny on their next visit to her bedside.

'At school,' said Henny.

'I want another clean nightgown.'

'I'll get you one,' said Lucy.

'You don't know which to bring. Maxine does all that,' said Cecilia, testily.

'How do you feel?' asked Henny.

'Perfectly well, thank you.'

'So you don't mind being here?'

'Why should I? It seems, Sister tells me, I had a little touch of pneumonia. I'm getting better as fast as I can. They need the bed for people who are really ill. Look at that poor old thing in the next bed.' The poor old thing pointed to was a good ten years younger than Cecilia.

'I brought you some fruit,' said Lucy.

Cecilia examined the offering. 'I'll keep a banana. Can't manage an apple. Thank you just the same. The food here, as a matter of fact, is delicious.' Tea came round at that moment. Fish fingers and peas.

It was almost six o'clock when Henny got home. She very much wanted to tell Jack about Cecilia, so she rang the office at once, half-hoping he might have left and be on the way home. But he was there, still working. 'I take it you won't be home tonight, then?' She said nothing about having called earlier.

'No darling. Sorry. I'll be down for the weekend, though, definitely.'

'The trains are running and the roads have been completely cleared.'

'I know. It isn't that. It's just that I've got an awful lot on.'

'You sound a bit worried.' As well you might, thought Henny, if you've let Kevin Preston-Jackson anywhere near you. 'But what I really wanted to tell you is that your old friend Cecilia is in hospital. I know she'd like to see you. But the weekend will do.'

'Look, I've got someone with me at the moment. I'll call you later.'

'She's got pneumonia.'

'Fine. Well, 'bye for now sweetheart.'

Henny put down the receiver and stood looking at it for a long time.

The someone who was with Jack was indeed Kevin Preston-Jackson, awaiting Jack's signature on his expense accounts. He dropped them on the desk as one who would say 'Sorry to bother you with trivia', lit a cigarette and turned away.

Jack's instinct was to sign the things as quickly as possible. It was a bit embarrassing, a guy who had fallen from the position of not only signing his own expenses but those of others as well. He had, in fact, scribbled his name on the bills before his eye caught the horrendous amounts. 'Bit steep?' he queried, gruffly.

Kevin picked up the bill in question. 'Oh that. Joyful Soap.

You know what soap people are. Whole bloody evening, it took me.'

'Oh well, if it keeps the client happy.'

Kevin smiled modestly. 'They seem pretty happy, I must say. In fact, I'm fairly certain we'll get the Face-Fresh business as well.' Face-Fresh was a new liquid soap that Jack had been slowly, cautiously pitching for, for months.

'Let's hope so,' was all he said.

He didn't leave London until Saturday morning. He had, for the remainder of the week, out-stayed Kevin every evening. He refused to admit to himself that this was because the Managing Director always stayed late. What did it matter, on Thursday, that the MD should put his head round the door and say 'Oh Jack! You still here? I was just going to have a word with Kevin. You made a good choice there.'

His spirits rose on the train. It was Saturday morning. He switched off the week behind him, like a sensible man. Now all he hoped was that the car would start, left, as it had been, in the station car park all week. He did not see, until he got to the door, that it had been vandalised. Window smashed, front tyres gone. He telephoned the police, who made notes and went away again. Then he took a taxi home.

Henny was making her first cheese soufflé, in celebration of her husband's arrival. Hearing a car draw up, she popped the soufflé in the oven and ran to the window to see Jack paying for the ride. 'Don't ask me about it,' he snapped.

Henny did not snap back. She poured him a glass of wine, juggled him over to the fireside, almost ruined the soufflé by opening the oven door twice, and tossed a salad in the dressing she had learnt to make after the ghastly experience of the sick-flavoured muck from the shop. She was rewarded.

'It's great to be home.'

'It's great to have you home. I hate to think of you staying in a hotel, alone.'

'I don't really mind it. And I'd rather be alone if I can't be with you.'

'I'd thought it would be nicer for you to use the flat.'

'Not really. I couldn't bear it, without you there. Home's where you are.'

Now that the soufflé, which had held up miraculously, was out of the way, Henny permitted herself to relax. She poured another glass of wine for both of them and pulled Jack down on to the hearthrug. She'd even learnt how to get the fire to give a good blaze. 'Ah,' said Jack, 'that's better. I'm almost glad you aren't pregnant yet. You aren't, are you?'

'I thought you wanted a baby.'

'I do. But I'd have to take care not to push it out of place, wouldn't I? Oh, Henny, my Henny.' Henny felt blissfully happy. 'This is the only place I want to be.'

'Me, too.'

Jack sat up. 'Which brings me to a point. We don't use the flat at all, do we? I know it's yours, and it's up to you what we do about it. But don't you think it would be more sensible to put it on the market?'

'I suppose you're right. And it would give us some capital, for sure. I mean, supposing things went wrong for you at WTS. Or, I mean, suppose you wanted to make a change.'

'Whatever makes you say that?'

'Oh, nothing. It's just that I'd like you to feel free. And the flat's all I can contribute, now. But, it's just that we were so happy there. Still, that was then, wasn't it?'

'I know how you feel. We *were* happy there. But we've moved on.'

'You're right. OK, let's do it. Do you want me to get an agent?'

'No need. I'll do it. If you're sure you don't mind. It's easier for me to do it, I'm on the spot and I'll put Glenda to work finding a good agent. Now tell me, what's this about Cecilia?'

'She's got pneumonia. I thought you weren't listening, when I rang you about it.'

Jack felt guilty. He knew he had only been half paying attention. 'Is that serious?' he now asked.

'She's getting better. I thought we'd go and see her in the hospital. She'd be so pleased. But damn, no car. I'll ring your mother and ask her. And I really will get some driving lessons and take the test. It's all my fault, the car. You should never have had to leave it at the station.'

★

'You look well, my boy,' said Cecilia, sitting up and looking round the ward to make sure everyone could see she had lots of visitors. Henny and Jack and Lucy, and Peter Dormer had come along as well.

'I am,' said Jack. 'It's having a good wife that does it.' He leant over and kissed Henny. How he loved her and how nice it would be to be driven to the station in the morning, kissed goodbye and met in the evening.

'You seem to have grown,' said Cecilia.

'I don't think so. It's because you're lying down.'

'I am not,' said Cecilia, straightening up vigorously and settling her nightgown.

After the hospital visit, Lucy and Peter came into Henny and Jack's house for drinks. While making the soufflé, Henny had grated too much cheese, so she'd gone for broke and made a batch of cheese straws. 'You certainly do have a good wife, Jack,' said Peter.

In bed on Sunday morning, Henny said 'Tell me a bit about things at the agency.'

'Not a lot to tell.'

'Darling, I do know a little about the business. OK, so it turns out I'm a red-hot cheese-straw cook but I'm not brain dead. When I rang you at the office last Wednesday, there was something on your mind. Client trouble?'

'No, no. Joyful Soap's going well, and it looks as though we might get Face-Fresh as well.'

'Face-Fresh? But that's marvellous. I never wanted to work on it myself but it would be a terrific account for you. Well done.'

'We haven't got it yet.'

'What do you mean? They must have talked to you.' As Jack remained silent for so long, she rallied courage enough to be devious. 'Is your new assistant working out all right?'

'Yes. Quite well. The MD thinks highly of him and so does Glenda.'

Henny got out of bed. 'I'll go and make some tea and toast.' She had heard all she needed to hear. She took breakfast back to bed, where they stayed all morning.

★

On Monday, Lucy turned up at seven o'clock to take her son to the railway station.

Promptly at 9.32, Henny made a telephone call. 'Jack Dormer, please,' she said and got, as she had expected she might, the redoubtable Glenda, who did not say 'Jack Dormer's office,' when she answered. What she said was 'Hello-ho.'

'Jack Dormer, please.' She raised her voice a couple of tones and introduced a sharp, bossy note she would never have used in her working days.

'Who is calling?'

Henny went ahead with her decision. 'Rena Bushell.'

'And what is this in connection with?'

'I wish to speak to Mr Dormer.'

'I'm sorry, he's not here yet. He doesn't usually get in until quite late on a Monday.'

Henny, now assuming the role of Miss Rena Bushell, brand manager of an American pizza-purveying company, added an impatient note. 'Then give me someone. I am looking for an advertising agency.'

Honeyed tones ensued. 'No problem. I'll put you straight through to Mr Preston-Jackson. He'll look after you.'

Kevin put out his cigarette in one of Glenda's plant-pots. His smoking habit was the only thing Glenda didn't like about him but she had plans to cure that.

'Hallo. Preston-Jackson. Kevin.'

'I really wanted to speak to Mr Jack Dormer.'

''Fraid he's not here. Lives in the country. But we're a team. And you are Tina Bushell. I've heard your name, I know I have.'

Encouraged by this patent lie, Henny warmed to her task and managed to put on the voice of an ambitious and flattered young female executive. 'Pizzas On Wheels. We're a fairly new franchise. Great stuff, though, American backing. We need an advertising agency.' She opened up further. This is a big chance for me. I'm quite young. Big break, you understand.'

'I do indeed. I'm sure I can help. Hang on a tick, will you? I'm just getting my secretary to switch in. Switch in, will you, Glenda? Don't want to miss important facts.'

'We're going to get big. At present we're based in Slough.'

Henny heard Kevin gulp. 'We're there because factory space is so cheap, you see. We're into massive production. I hope you don't think we're too small for you at the moment. I can only commit £200,000 right now.' She almost fell off her chair at the next gulp. 'What I suggest is that the first thing you should do is to come and see us at work.'

'Be delighted,' said Kevin, lulled into condescension.

'Is £200,000 too small for you?'

'Not in the least. Many of the best campaigns start small. Would you give Glenda directions? I'm just off to a meeting. I'll drive out. When would suit you?'

'Eleven forty-five tomorrow morning. Sorry to rush you, I hope you can fit it in, but I really want to get under way.'

'OK. Bye for now, Tina.'

'Rena.' Henny couldn't resist the teasing interjection. She needn't have bothered. It was difficult not to burst out laughing.

'OK, Tina, look forward to meeting you.'

'Tell him,' said Henny to Glenda, 'to go out on the motorway east until he gets to the housing estate, pass that and go on to the industrial estate. Go through that, turn right. Turn right again and then left. We've already planted some fir trees in front of the factory so he can look out for those. Have you got all that?'

'Yes,' said Glenda.

'Don't forget the fir trees!' Having put the telephone down, grinning more hugely than she had for weeks, she picked it up again and called the driving school. 'I'll take six lessons, to start with. I would like to begin today.'

'Oh, I don't know about today,' came a nail-examining voice.

'It's today or I go elsewhere.'

The driving tutor picked her up at 12.30. By the end of the lesson, he had to admit that he was impressed by the rapidity with which his pupil had learnt to change gear. 'Most ladies who haven't driven before,' he said, sitting beside Henny outside her front door and hoping he might get invited in for coffee, 'ask for automatic.'

'Do they? I really don't know whether my husband's car is automatic or what. I know very little about cars. Except that as I intend to buy one for myself, I wish to be able to find the best value I can get in an old car. So I had better be able to use grown-ups' gears, hadn't I?' She gave him a dazzling smile. The instructor admired her legs as she put them on the ground. Closing the door and looking at him through the window, Henny concluded, 'And I wish to pass the test first time. See you in two days.'

'Bet she's not as cold as she looks,' said the instructor to himself, slipping reluctantly into the driving seat. 'Just my luck. The ones you fancy won't give you the time of day.'

12

Cecilia got home sooner than expected. 'I'd keep her like a shot,' said Sister, 'if I thought it was best. But in her case, it isn't.'

'Are you sure?' asked Lucy. 'She's told me you need the bed.'

'I do. Heaven knows, I do. But I promise you, that's not why. She wants to be home. And she has a right to be home.'

'What if she falls? In the night, maybe, when none of us is there?'

'She may. I don't say she won't. The way she is at the moment, I'd say she'd pick herself up again. She's like that. We'll miss her, as a matter of fact. She's quite a revelation. I haven't been long in this hospital.'

Ah, thought Lucy, this must be why she has never heard of The Elms.

'I haven't had much to do with comfortably off old people,' Sister went on. 'I was in Birmingham, before. Nowhere to go, for most of them. But your friend Mrs Boxendale is as gutsy an old biddy as ever I ran across.'

Cecilia spurned a wheelchair and walked out of the hospital on Lucy's arm.

Jack had actually been deeply upset when first he saw Mrs Boxendale in the hospital. Of course she was old, he knew that. But the possibility of her dying was not to be thought of. He had no idea of the aches and pains and humiliations of old age. But Sister had cheered him up no end with her optimism, almost as though she shared his belief in Cecilia's immortality, almost as though an old woman twenty-five years past the biblical three score and ten was really a tree that would go on forever putting out new leaves.

He went back to London and to work, in a contented frame of mind. He walked from Charing Cross to the office, thinking about Henny, so clearly happy with their home. Her generous agreement to sell her flat was final proof of that.

Arriving at WTS, he entered the lift and wondered why his restored spirits were sinking as it carried him up to his floor. Glenda was watering her ghastly plants. There was no sign of Kevin Preston-Jackson. He entered his own office, hung his coat up carefully, sat down and buzzed Glenda. 'Please tell Mr Preston-Jackson I want to see him.'

'Yes,' said Glenda. 'Would you like some coffee?'

'Thank you. But no milk and no sugar. And, Glenda, I want you to find a good estate agent. I'm putting my flat on the market. Find an agent who knows the market. The flat is in Covent Garden.'

'I know it is,' said Glenda. For her, this was good news. If Jack was about to sell the flat, that must mean Henny was finally out of the way. 'Would you like me to deal with this?' she enquired, her thoughts turning to promotion. Already she could see herself as office manager.

'Yes. Get going, will you, please. I'm going up now to see the MD.' Unaccountably cheered, Jack strode up to the MD's office, freedom in his step.

He had arranged to stay the next couple of nights in the same hotel as before. Thank goodness this would only be necessary until his car was fixed and he could get to and from the station. Perhaps perversely, he paid for it himself. Having no car was not quite the same as snow on the railway line. And Preston-Jackson's phenomenal expense accounts had reinforced his own honesty.

He enquired mildly, on Tuesday, as to the whereabouts of his assistant.

'Didn't he tell you?' said Glenda. 'I expect he meant to. New client. He's gone out to a meeting. New factory, somewhere. Going to be big.'

Jack went to see Stan Howard. 'Don't nag me,' said Stan. 'Your new man's demanded copy for Face-Fresh. We're doing our best.'

On the Wednesday Kevin appeared, keeping his end up,

bustling into Jack's office, straight past Glenda without respond-
ing to her smile. 'What a day. The woman must be mad.'

'What woman?' asked Jack patiently.

'Oh, you know. They're like that, women. Delusions of
grandeur. I blame this feminism lark.'

'Please tell me what has happened,' Jack said firmly.

'Oh some woman, Tina something. Got me to go out and
see a pizza factory, £200,000 budget,' said Kevin from his
disadvantaged position in the low chair on the non-managerial
side of Jack's desk.

'So?' asked Jack.

'Fraud. Total fraud. Really, some people. I don't know what
the world's coming to.'

'Any news on Face-Fresh?' asked Jack.

'Well . . .' began Kevin.

Jack looked at his watch. 'Oh sorry, I'll have to stop you
now. Bad luck about the dud client. Can happen. Better luck
with Face-Fresh.' He then kept silence. Kevin, whose legs were
not his best friends in the mornings, was obliged to pull himself
up and leave the room.

Cecilia was not aware how lucky she was to be approaching
spring in her own home. She knew nothing about old ladies
turned out of hospital to the empty bewilderment of a cold
room. Very soon she took Maxine's ministrations totally for
granted. 'That figure of a young man with a bird in his hand.
It is in the wrong position,' she would announce, glaring at the
mantelpiece.

'Sorry, Mrs Boxendale. I moved it while I was dusting,' said
Maxine.

'Don't drop it,' said Mrs Boxendale, falling into her chair.

'Have a sherry,' said Maxine. As far as she was concerned, if
Mrs Boxendale was able to get round and be testy, then Mrs
Boxendale was all right and *that* was all right.

The snow had melted away. In the gardens of Tiddingfold,
the bulbs began to show their shoots. Dot Blunt, more and
more frequently, walked up to Mrs Boxendale's house, her little
feet booted. Like many plump women, she had feet and ankles
as graceful as those of a Jersey cow. Major Blunt continued to

glare over his pink gin and upbraid her for drunkenness. She had the greatest respect for him but she was a lot happier up at Mrs Boxendale's. 'You're marvellous,' said Maxine. 'You always get her to eat a bit of something.'

Henny passed her driving test in February.

In March, one of those tricksy periods of early sunshine awoke the tortoise. Lucy heard a scratching at the shed door. She had had a happy morning.

Now that she could allow herself to admit it, she had been worrying, ever since Christmas, about Henny. Henny and Jack, of course, but really Henny. But this morning had soothed her mind. She had been to see Cecilia and found Henny there.

It was about half-past eleven when Lucy knocked on Cecilia's door. Maxine let her in. 'Sorry, Lady Lucy. I hope I didn't keep you waiting. We was all laughing.'

'Shouldn't you be at school?' asked Lucy.

'Off sick,' said Maxine brazenly, her cheeks rosy. In her self-elected role as personal assistant to Mrs Boxendale, she had dispensed with her white makeup, though not with her exciting coiffures. Mrs Boxendale, bless her, got a lot of fun out of asking, 'What colour tomorrow, Maxine?'

Lucy stood, unnoticed for a moment, at the sitting-room door. Cecilia was sitting forward in her chair. 'Did you really? Oh Henny, I wish I'd ever done something like that. A wild-goose chase, what fun. What did you say the man's name is? Preston-Jackson? Sounds a complete charlatan. Mind you, I've nothing against double-barrelled names, some of my best friends have them. But there aren't that many genuine ones and my guess is that that one is not. A charlatan.'

'He is,' said Henny. 'Believe me, I know. Oh Lucy, hallo, how lovely. I was just telling Cecilia about a bit of fun I had.'

'And I was envying her,' said Cecilia. 'In all my life, I never did a thing like that.'

'You did lots of things I never did,' said Henny.

'Yes. Well, I suppose so. But it's the things you didn't do and never will that you regret.'

Dot Blunt came in from the kitchen. 'Mrs Boxendale, dear, I've left one of those little chicken patties for you. You liked it the last time, but you needn't bother with it if you don't fancy it. Maxine can always take it home, can't you, Maxine? Ooh, a sherry, thanks. I could just do with that. Hallo, Lady Lucy, how are you?'

'Have you seen Mrs Dormer's car, Lady Lucy?' said Maxine. 'It's vintage; one of them vintage cars.' Maxine's idea of 'vintage' was somewhat governed by her own age. 'She bought it herself. I mean, I know Mr Dormer would give her anything, but she bought it herself. It's, what is it? Oh, I know . . . MG Midget. Two-seater, open sports. Isn't that right, Mrs Dormer?'

'Quite right,' said Henny.

'Could have had that Ford Escort XR3i convertible or the Fiat X19.' Maxine looked admiringly at Henny.

'Maxine knows more about cars than I do,' said Henny.

Maxine nodded sagely. One day, she thought, one day. She admired Henny greatly. 'You got the best one, I'll tell you. Mind you, I did like the idea of the Ford Escort, but four seats? No, you want your own, you do.'

So Lucy was, of course, pleased. Her big worry, all along, was that Tiddingfold would drive Henny out. How could a girl like Henny endure the daily tedium that was the life-blood of a slow-thinking, slow-acting village? But with her own car and especially a car spectacularly unsuitable to meals on wheels or hospital lifts, the signs were good. She was not ashamed to admit to herself that she would miss Henny dreadfully, if things didn't work out.

It was almost one o'clock when Maxine and Lucy became aware that Cecilia was flagging. Lucy asked to see the car, and went out with Henny. Maxine came too and demonstrated its exciting open top. 'Must go, now, though. Got to get Mrs Boxendale to have a lay-down.' Lucy and Henny smiled after Maxine and stood talking by the car.

'Hallo, Mrs Boxendale. I'm indoors again,' Maxine re-entered the house. 'I'm ever so bossy. Hope you don't mind.' Cecilia allowed herself to be settled under a rug, her feet on a footstool. 'You can have the telly, if you want,' said Maxine. 'I'll just nip out and say goodbye to Lady Lucy.'

'Maxine,' said Lucy, 'you are very good. You knew just when she'd had enough.'

'Well, she was a bit tired. Not through you. But we had that

Mrs Phillips in this morning. Interfering old bat. Her and her Elms. Henny got rid of her double quick. Marvellous, Henny is. You'll have to excuse me, I'm just going to walk home with Mrs Blunt.'

So it was in a happy frame of mind that Lucy drove home and, wandering round her garden, heard the scratching of Heraclitus's impatient claw on the shed door. 'Well, my dear chap,' she said, as the solemn reptile stumbled out and settled down on the path to look about him. 'So it's spring, is it?' She put her finger under his chin and rubbed gently. His skin was in silky, perfect order, no scaling. Good for cod-liver oil and that special food Henny had brought him last year. She must get some more of that.

Heraclitus made his gracious progress down the path. He permitted Lucy to sit down and take him into her lap. After a while, clouds scudded across the sky and it was suddenly cold. She carried him into the shed and put him down by his box of hay and leaves. Then she went into the house and boiled an egg, so as to cut off the white part for his supper. He was nodding when she took it to him. He fell asleep with his beak on the goodie. She closed the door.

The following morning the sun shone again and Lucy went out to the shed to release the impatient and strengthening Heraclitus. He almost bounded out.

An hour later, she found him in the driveway with his shell broken. It was not just a crack but an irreparable, dented break. There was no knowing how it had happened. It mattered not whether he had been run over by the postman's van or the milkman's. Whatever the cause, he was finished. Lucy knelt down beside her shattered pet. Hearing her voice, Heraclitus made an effort and put his head out. There was gentle despair in his glazed eyes. Lucy stroked his soft throat. She put him on a piece of blanket in a box and talked to him all the way to the vet's. 'Don't worry, old boy. I'll make it better soon. Don't be frightened.'

At the vet's, she took him out of the blanket and settled him down on her lap in the waiting-room. His clawed foot rested on her finger. A spaniel reached up and sniffed at him as though he was meat and Lucy was filled with rage at the owner for not calling the dog away. But she remained quiet. She did not wish to scream with anger and frighten her little friend in these terminal minutes of his life.

The vet said, 'You can sometimes repair shells. But I'm afraid there's too much damage to this poor fellow. The shell of a tortoise is its ribcage and I'm afraid this has been badly crushed. I'm sorry, but he won't survive it.'

'He'll die?' asked Lucy. 'Then will you put him to sleep at once? As you would for a dog or a cat.'

'He will just die. If I do as you ask, I'm afraid it will cost £12 plus VAT, I have to tell you. People think we overcharge.'

'Please,' said Lucy.

'They're nice creatures, aren't they?' The vet was about to carry Heraclitus away but Lucy said, 'I'll come with you, if you please. I would prefer to hold him.' Heraclitus died in her arms.

'I'll dispose, shall I?' asked the vet.

'What?'

'Sometimes people want to bury their own pets. I think up in a puff of smoke is better.'

As Lucy re-entered Alexandra Lodge, carrying the scrap of blanket that last had held Heraclitus, the telephone rang. She was glad of the interruption; it would take her out of the ridiculous grief she was suffering over the death of a so-called cold-blooded creature. It was Penelope.

Penelope had just got back from her check-up. The baby was, so far, in the right position but Penelope had got to be careful. Lucy couldn't be quite sure whether the baby was too big or too small. By the same token, she wasn't entirely sure whether Penelope was for or against epidurals. She daren't admit that she didn't quite know what an epidural was but she was quite sure it wasn't twilight sleep.

Brian, it seemed, was being recalcitrant about his duty to be present at the birth. Lucy shuddered as she listened to Penelope's complaints. It was impossible to explain that the last thing she would have wanted, in labour, was the presence of dear nice Peter. If Peter had been in at the birth of Jack, it was a dead certainty that Penelope would never have been conceived. 'Are you sure you want Brian there?' she asked cautiously.

'He ought to be. I mean, look at me. My ankles.'

Penelope, thought Lucy, making appropriate noises before she rang off, would not be interested in hearing about the death of Heraclitus.

13

'It's so stupid.' Lucy, in Cecilia's sitting-room, made her third useless attempt to dry her eyes with a sodden handkerchief. 'Really, crying over a tortoise.'

'Oh, I don't know,' said Cecilia. 'I can quite see why one could get fond of a tortoise. Better than those thumping great labradors of Betty's. And then the puppies. Nice enough little creatures but so smelly. Henny dear, just pop upstairs, will you, and bring that box of tissues from beside my bed.' While Lucy wept, she chatted on, not to be listened to but to fill the air with sympathy. 'My father was keen on fox-terriers. And I was given a kitten. Pretty. Vile temper, though. Not like your nice Heraclitus. He was a mannerly creature. Ah, Henny. Here you are. Get us a glass of sherry, will you?'

'I've got the car,' said Lucy, drearily.

'Leave it here,' said Henny, not without some pride. 'You need a drink. I'll drive you home. We're all so sorry about Heraclitus.'

Cecilia drank her sherry. She and Lucy were not in the kissing habit so she just put out her old hand and patted her friend. Drawing it back and looking at it, she touched her own face and added, 'I'm glad you were so fond of him. I look a bit like him myself, don't I?' At last Lucy laughed. Between them, Cecilia and Henny persuaded her to drink another glass. When, later, Henny took her home, Cecilia went to the window to wave. She rather hoped Henny would soon take her for another spin in the dashing little car. She stumped back to the television, chuckling to herself 'No room in that little vehicle for a child-seat. Child-seat, indeed. That's Penelope's sort of thing, not Henny's.'

The advance of April and the arrival of May were good for Cecilia. She could get out into her garden. Unseen by her, Dot Blunt would watch anxiously out of the window as she abandoned her walking stick and pulled at the weeds, panting and gasping.

'She'll fall, Maxine.'

'The ground's soft.'

'You mean, don't interfere.'

'I wouldn't be so cheeky, Mrs Blunt. I wish you'd tell me how to make that kipper pâté. She liked that.'

Dot burst out laughing. 'You do mean don't interfere. I won't, don't worry.'

Early in May, Henny had a telephone call. 'Hallo, Henny, it's Glenda.'

'Hallo, Glenda, how are you?' Henny hoped Jack was all right. Now that she was, to Jack's secretary, merely a wife, such a communication was unexpected.

Having gone through all the 'Fine, thanks, and how are you?' preliminaries, Glenda informed her that the estate agent had found a very promising potential buyer for her flat. A buyer, it seemed, with enough money to pay almost the full asking price. 'I've shown it to them myself.'

'That was very helpful of you, Glenda.'

'Yes. Well, they like it. They want to have another look.'

'So let them.'

'That's the problem. Jack can't spare me.'

Refraining from asking whether Glenda meant Jack or Kevin, Henny merely said, 'I see. So you'd like me to do it? Very well. I'll make arrangements.'

'I've got a key.'

'That won't be necessary. I have one myself.'

'Will you let the estate agent know what you decide, then?'

'Certainly. Goodbye, Glenda.'

Now that the sale looked like becoming a reality, Henny wanted to know exactly who it was who planned to make her old home theirs. She and Jack had been so happy there. More than that, she had earned it herself. A long time ago. They'd just better be appreciative!

Two days later, she telephoned Stan Howard. 'Well, you at last,' said Stan.

'I'm coming up to London. Want to give me lunch?'

'You planning to run away with me? I'm game, but do you think Jack and my old lady will get on together?' Stan was given to quips.

'Can you manage Thursday?'

'Let's see. Thursday. Award ceremony at the Dorchester, and the managing director wants to talk to me afterwards; he plans I should get the first knighthood for contributions to pulp advertising. I can cancel all that.' Faced with silence, he added, 'Henny? You gone slow or something? Thursday's great, you silly cow. Meet me at the Three Greyhounds.'

'Where's that?'

'You *are* out of touch. Corner of Old Compton Street and Greek. One o'clock. Don't be late.'

Henny went through her wardrobe. Almost everything in it was not exactly too tight, it was just that it did not hang loose. Her legs were all right, though. Tights, and stand up straight, that was the answer.

She was not quite sure why it was that she didn't tell Jack she was going up to town. She drove him to the station, still freshly satisfied with her ability to do so. But still she felt guilty as she bade him goodbye and left the station. Guilty and puzzled. She'd be much better off if she sold it. Her own money in her own bank account. Almost like the days of having a salary. Why couldn't she explain all that to Jack, instead of sneaking off and waiting half an hour before catching the next train? She put the car in the station car park, praying it wouldn't be broken into in her absence.

Arrived at the flat, she let herself in with the key she had always, without thinking about it, kept. It had been in her handbag ever since the day she'd left. The buyer was punctual. Buyers, actually. A young woman and a young man.

They were, Henny at once recognised, totally suited to her flat and it to them. The young woman was particularly appealing. She was the one who queried the selling price and tried to get it knocked down. At the same time, it was not hard to see that she was positively stroking Henny's erstwhile home. 'I do like it, Mrs Dormer. I'm only bargaining because one is supposed to, these days, isn't one?'

'One is,' said Henny, touching her old walls.

'If you want it, sweetheart, we'll have it,' said the young man.

'Only for the full selling price,' said Henny. 'Think it over. You can call the agent. I'll have to leave, I've got another appointment.'

'Can we go on looking round alone?' asked the young man.

'No, sorry. I'm locking up.'

On the way out, the young couple, who, as Henny could well see, desperately wanted the flat, became communicative. 'We can go for the price, don't worry about that. We're both in advertising, you see.'

They parted company in Long Acre. 'Maybe she doesn't like advertising people,' said the young man as Henny strode rapidly away. 'People don't. When they don't know anything about it.'

'She does,' said the young woman. 'If I'm not mistaken, she was once Henny Brack. She wouldn't remember, but she interviewed me when I came out of college. I often wondered what became of her.'

'OK,' said Stan, having embraced Henny affectionately. The copper-topped table he had appropriated in a quiet corner of the Three Greyhounds was already supplied with a bottle of white wine and one of mineral water. 'So what brings you to the metropolis?'

'I've been showing my flat to a trendy young couple. They want to buy it. The first offer I've had.'

'So you're taking it?'

Henny drank a glass of wine, waved away the mineral water, refilled her glass and said, 'Funny you should ask that.'

'Have a cigarette,' said Stan, passing his pack of whatever-you-can-get-cheapest.

Henny, looking around her and breathing in the atmosphere, took the first of three.

'So how,' enquired Stan deviously, 'is Tiddingfold? I went to see your mother the other day, incidentally.'

'Did you, Stan? You are good.'

'No I'm not. I like her. But she's got it all wrong about you. Let's not go into that at the moment. You want anything to eat? They have good fishcakes.'

'How's your family, Stan?'

'All right, thanks. My daughter's just left her husband.'

'She's old enough to be married?'

Stan muddled his fishcake up with his cigarette. 'She's not far short of you. Well, she's twenty-six.'

'So what's gone wrong?'

'She lived with him for two years. Nice enough young bloke. Then they got married. Big wedding. My wife did everything: marquee, flowers. We've got a nice back garden in Bromley, I'll give myself that. Sylvia – ' Stan took a healthy swallow of his wine – 'Sylvia was pleased. She's old-fashioned. She really put herself out.'

'So what happened? Was he unfaithful?'

'Not on your life. Faithful unto death, mortgage and dinner at seven. He's a nice chap, dependable too, which is more than you can say for some blokes. She bolted. Don't know why. I've always worked my arse off, so I don't know what figures, with my kids. She's gone off to find space, is what she says.'

'I know what she means,' said Henny.

'But you're all right. Happy as a pig in clover, so I gather.'

'Yes.'

Stan ordered a second bottle of wine. 'So that's good. Ever thought of doing some freelance? I could use you.'

'That's nice of you, Stan, but you know it never works. At least, not the way I do ads. Did, I mean.'

'True. I miss you, though. If ever you decide to come back, your desk'll be ready.'

'But I could hardly come back to WTS. I mean, think about it.'

'Because you're a bigger name than Jack? Well, you are. Jack knows that himself. He doesn't begrudge it, he's not a petty man. In fact, he's a generous man. A bit too generous for his own good at times, but that's another story.'

'You mean Kevin Preston-Jackson?'

'I do. But he got a bit of a come-uppance a little while ago. *Someone* played a very naughty trick on him. I wonder who?'

Henny looked demure. 'It was a wet day, too. But you're right, Stan, Jack is a generous man. But don't you think, if what you say about me is true – and I don't mind telling you I'm not so sure of my talents these days – it wouldn't work? I am his wife and wives aren't supposed to be the successes. Well, at least not in the same agency.'

'Has Jack said so?'

'No-o.'

Stan changed the subject, mentally ticking himself off for his old trick of stirring it after the fourth glass. 'It must be lovely, now, in your part of the world.'

'It is. It's a totally different world. But it's got good values. I'm very fond of Jack's mother. And Mrs Boxendale, she's a lovely old lady, she lives three doors away from us. And there's a nice kid, Maxine, who helps her and I like her very much, and there's Mrs – '

'And you've lost your cutting edge . . .'

'Blunt,' concluded Henny.

'Sounds thrilling,' said Stan.

'Don't be sarcastic. There are far worse places to live, believe me.'

'Very well.'

'Why don't you come and see for yourself? Why don't you and Sylvia come down one Sunday to lunch? I want to get Ma down for a few days, so you could come when she's with us and you'd get something decent to eat.'

Stan upended the bottle. Henny could see him debating another. Long habit with Stan said now was the moment to get him back to work. He could stand up and show no sign after two bottles, but three were out of the question. She stood up. 'We're off, then, are we?' he said.

'I've got to go and talk to the estate agent.' Henny watched Stan walk away. Half a mile's walk and he'd be sharp as a tack again. No good regretting that she wasn't going with him.

She set off in the direction of the estate agent's office. But her legs wouldn't take her there. Making for Charing Cross, she thought mistily, 'My legs are like Lavinia's hand, in *Androcles and the Lion*. When she couldn't reach out and throw the sacrificial offering on the altar, even to please that nice Roman soldier. Oh dear, better have a sleep in the train.'

There was no sense in driving all the way home from the station and then having to go back later for Jack. In any case, she'd had far too much wine. She spent the next three hours walking round Ashden, thinking what an exceedingly dull town it was.

The next day she had an aggrieved telephone call from the estate agent. 'They want the flat. They'll pay full price. I thought you were coming in yesterday afternoon. They were waiting for you.'

'I'm sorry,' said Henny. 'I was delayed on business and I hadn't time before my train went.'

'I see. Their offer holds. I strongly advise you to take it.'

'Let me think about it. I need more time.'

14

At the end of May, Penelope gave birth to a son. She was Dr Phillips's favourite mummy, having no desire for such nonsenses as underwater birth or, worse still, giving birth at home. She got even better marks for just the right amount of post-natal depression. She and Dr Phillips spent a satisfactory quarter of an hour exchanging satisfactorily old-fashioned words, such as 'weepy' and 'baby-blues'. A nice chat with Mrs Phillips, they both agreed, would do her all the good in the world. Keeping his masterful wife busy and, at the same time, himself less so, was the work of Dr Phillips's life.

Penelope trotted off, smiling up at him admiringly as he escorted her to the surgery door and bade her goodbye with an avuncular pat on the back.

The baby was brought to see Mrs Boxendale. Penelope did the old lady the great favour of putting it on her lap. Maxine came to the rescue and heaved the windy blob of humanity up on her own shoulder.

'I don't really like them at that age,' confided Mrs Boxendale, after Maxine had got rid of the proud mother and her son and heir.

'Neither do I,' said Maxine, with a shudder. 'Last thing I'd want one of.'

'Mrs Phillips tells me you girls have babies to get council housing.'

'Not me. We got council housing, anyway. Always have had. And it's enough looking after my dad, never mind a blooming baby. You ask my mum. She'd have a fit if I did anything like that. She didn't want my last little brother, not that she doesn't like him now he's here. But she could of done without him. Oh no, not me.'

Maxine kept her opinion of Mrs Phillips to herself. Always poking her nose in. If she had her way, Mrs Phillips wouldn't be let in the house.

As it happened, Mrs Boxendale was almost always alone when Mrs Phillips made her forays. Usually in the afternoon, when Henny, Lucy, Dot Blunt and Maxine had come and gone, the very time when she could find Mrs Boxendale in a doze. She now openly addressed Mrs Boxendale by her Christian name. Henny had long done so, but only at Mrs Boxendale's invitation. Maxine didn't: the very idea would have shocked her. Cecilia had become very fond indeed of Maxine, almost more intimate with her than with anyone. But it was an intimacy unspoken. Maxine had got into the way of giving the private, practical attentions that were becoming increasingly necessary. Sometimes she petted Mrs Boxendale with familiar hands but never with familiar address.

'So when did Mrs Phillips tell you about girls like me,' now asked Maxine, 'since she seems to know so much about it?'

'I don't remember. I'd like to walk round the garden, please.'

'It's just not sensible,' said Mrs Phillips to Mrs Merritt. 'Her going on in that house, all alone. She can't manage, you know. Between ourselves, there's incontinence there.'

'Oh dear.' Mrs Merritt had heard Mrs Phillips on the subject of Cecilia's incontinence many times. Intending to be helpful, she now enquired, 'Are you planning to make her go into The Elms?'

'That's a funny way of putting it,' said Mrs Phillips crossly. 'I'm not planning anything. I'm merely trying to help in a sphere I understand.' Mrs Merritt looked apologetic. 'The Elms,' drove home Mrs Phillips, 'is full. Goodness knows, I'd have my work cut out to get her on the waiting list.' Mrs Merritt forbore to mention something her husband had said about The Elms not being all that full at all. It had to do, if she'd got it right – she never listened when he talked sums she didn't understand – with the difficulty the old folks had in selling their houses to pay the fees.

'The Elms is lovely, though,' she said, placatingly. 'Just the gardens alone.'

And now Marijke had agreed to abandon her neighbourhood duties for a few days, and pay Tiddingfold a visit. After a couple of false starts, Henny finally pinned her down to the end of June. 'And don't change your mind, Ma, there's a dear. I'm asking some friends specially for while you're with me. Stan and Sylvia. I've promised them some decent food, so you see I need you!'

'So that's the reason you're asking me,' said Marijke severely, and thoroughly gratified. She arrived with her usual travelling delicatessen, richly scenting the hot air of Ashden station.

Having set out early, Marijke spent the morning in Henny's kitchen. After lunch, she put on her good shoes and paid a call on Mrs Boxendale. 'I usually look in during the morning,' said Henny.

'This,' said Marijke strictly, 'is a social call.' To the good shoes she had added her afternoon dress. She rang the front-door bell and was admitted by Mrs Phillips.

Cecilia was leaning back in her armchair, eyes drooping. Beside her, seated too close and neck out-thrust, was Mrs Merritt, giving advice. 'Now really, you may not like the idea, but what you ought to do is get some paper napkins. They make such nice ones these days.' Marijke wondered *why* Mrs Boxendale should get paper napkins. Mrs Merritt droned on: 'I got my own mother to get paper napkins. She jibbed, of course. She'd always used double-damask, naturally. But I said to her, without a maid any more . . .'

Mrs Boxendale rallied enough to open an eye and murmur, 'Double damask dinner napkins, dibble dabble danner nipkins.'

Mrs Phillips gave Marijke a significant look. 'Good afternoon, Mrs Boxendale,' said Marijke. 'Do you remember me? I am the mother of Henny.'

'Of course I remember you. It is a great pleasure to see you again. Please do sit down. Mrs Merritt is just leaving.'

Mrs Merritt almost stood up, but fought the last ditch. 'I was telling dear Cecilia what lovely paper napkins you can buy, these days. We can't have her starching linen ones, can we?'

Cecilia sat bolt upright. 'I will not have beastly paper napkins in this house.'

'But I was only trying to tell you about – '

'Paper napkins!' Almost a spit of contempt. 'Perhaps you, Mrs Merritt, have not heard of drip-dry? I recommend the invention. I have two dozen drip-dry napkins, quite enough to see me out, and Maxine puts them into the washing machine for me.'

Mrs Phillips stepped in. 'Quite right,' she said soothingly. 'I dislike paper napkins myself.' Not a qualm in her about shopping her best friend. 'We wouldn't dream of them at The Elms. Clean napkins every day, clean sheets every day. All drip-dry. Wonderful.'

'How did you find Cecilia?' asked Henny, who was out in her garden smoking when her mother returned.

'Old.'

'Want some tea, Ma? Just let me finish this cigarette and I'll come in and put on the kettle.'

Marijke very much wanted some tea. 'Why not finish it indoors?' she asked.

'Jack doesn't like it.'

This reply was totally acceptable to Marijke. Restored by tea, she sat at the kitchen table and said, 'That Mrs Phillips. She has plans. What is this The Elms?'

'It's her nursing home.'

'I have a feeling,' said Marijke, upon whom tea acted as an upper. 'Maybe its business is not too busy. She has her eye on Mrs Boxendale.'

'I'll be seeing you on Sunday, then,' said Stan to Jack on the Friday. Jack looked shifty. Stan laughed, 'Bet she's never said a word about inviting us. She rang Sylvia, you know.' This was perfectly true. But as Jack had made no mention of the day Henny came to town and had lunch with him, Stan made no mention of it either.

'Of course she did. She told me days ago. She arranged specially for while her mother is staying. She wants to do you proud.'

What Jack was unable to look Stan in the eye about was the head-hunter. Not so much the head-hunter – everyone knew that head-hunters were scrabbling round for business these days – no, it was his own reaction on this occasion.

He daren't admit, even to himself, that he had made a dreadful mistake in hiring Kevin Preston-Jackson. He couldn't blame the man for fighting to survive. But Kevin's fight for survival, though more subtle than the behaviour of the cuckoo, was nevertheless weakening Jack's prospects at WTS by the day. The managing director was almost besotted with him. Face-Fresh was now secure and entirely credited to Kevin, in spite of the previous months of Jack's careful nurturing.

The job on offer was one he wouldn't have considered a few months ago. It fell into the category of 'Terrific opportunity, Jack. A challenge.' In short, it was the managing directorship of a small, new advertising agency, who were offering an alarmingly large salary as long as they could get a reputable chap out of one of the good old establishments. And that chap, Jack was assured, was him. 'You're just what they're looking for. Sanders and Sanders. They're getting off the ground fast, you know.'

'Who *are* Sanders and Sanders?' asked Jack.

'Well, it's just Sanders, actually. Jeremy Sanders. Decided to twin the name, you know. Really bright, got lots of charisma.'

'I haven't,' said Jack.

'Ah. That's the point. The reputation, that's what you'd bring.'

Coming back to Stan, Jack enquired if he needed directions.

'I know the way,' said Stan. 'We used to bring the children down to Bay Sands when they were little. As soon as I could afford a car. Often drove through Tiddingfold. Pretty.'

The car that pulled up outside Mulberry Cottage on Sunday was a lot in advance of Stan's first Ford. That still didn't make it a Porsche. In truth, WTS would have accorded Stan Howard any car he chose. But a comfortable car that didn't go wrong was all he required.

Henny had laid the table for seven. Lucy and Peter were to join them. It was a lovely day; Jack had put the drinks tray in the garden. The only way into the garden was through the kitchen. Jack planned on french doors from the sitting-room. Henny had begged him to hang on a while. 'Let's put in a second bathroom first,' she had said. 'Good idea,' he had agreed, 'make it a family house.' Henny had said nothing about the addition to selling value of a second bathroom. Her thoughts were not as formulated as that.

Henny led Sylvia into the garden. 'We've lost Stan,' she said. 'I know what he's doing, he's stopped to talk to my ma. When we get the pair of them out I'll introduce you to her properly.' Now that she looked at Sylvia Howard, Henny was surprised. She realised she had expected a Mrs Tiggywinkle figure. She had even provided a bottle of sweet sherry.

Sylvia Howard seemed tall, though she was not as tall as she looked, and she had pretty legs. She asked for a spritzer. 'Stan's been so looking forward to coming,' she said, 'so don't let me drink too much. I'll be driving us home.'

Stan emerged. 'She doesn't want to join us just now, and we're in luck. We're in for a treat, if my eyes and nose are anything to go by. Thank you, Jack, that white wine looks perfect.'

In a few minutes, Lucy and Peter emerged from the kitchen door, Lucy carrying a bowl of something attractive and a plate of blackish slices to dip into it. 'Marijke said to bring this out,' she said. 'Hallo. Mrs Howard, I'm so very pleased to meet you at last. I'm Lucy Dormer. And this is my husband, Peter. I made friends with your husband at Henny and Jack's wedding.'

'I was so sorry not to be there. But my son had flu. Or I think it was flu.'

'One can never remember, can one? It's always something. My daughter's just had a baby, a little boy.'

'How lovely. I'd love to be a grandmother. But my daughter shows no signs.' Lucy and Sylvia settled down happily together.

When Marijke called the party to table, everyone was friends. It was, Henny could see, every woman's idea of a luncheon party going off well. Peter was seated between Sylvia and Lucy, who leant across him to address one another. 'Now you two, may a mere man get a word in?' he enquired jovially. Marijke, opposite him, was seeing that his plate was filled. He wasn't too sure about this food; Sunday ought to be him carving a joint. But manners made him taste, and tasting made him eat, with relish.

It was half-past three before Henny could escape to the kitchen and make the coffee. In the brief silence she utilised her main skill and carried out a big pot, for at last everyone had drifted into the garden.

'Bring the brandy, will you, darling?' called Jack. 'And the Cointreau. And there's some Tia Maria.'

'Got any Courvoisier, my boy?' asked Peter. 'Well done with the sweet liqueurs, by the way. The ladies like them. But give me a decent brandy any day.'

Jack brought his father a brandy and poured himself an undisguised Tia Maria. Peter raised an eyebrow but Jack smiled. Now that he was no longer daunted by his father, he would drink what he preferred in his own house.

Stan, unaware that he was going up in Peter Dormer's estimation, also took brandy. Cupping his balloon of the delicious stuff, he watched Sylvia and Lucy strolling round the garden with Marijke. 'Ladies like gardening,' he said. 'Maybe I will, one day. When I get time.' He was, and he knew it, a little drunk. Well, quite drunk. But Sylvia would get him home.

Henny sat alone, not with the ladies and not with the men. Stan and her father-in-law were getting along brilliantly, a good thing. She wondered if anyone would notice if she slipped out and went down the street to Cecilia's. 'Cointreau, darling?' asked Jack. Henny never drank Cointreau.

Sylvia came up and said, 'This has been a lovely party, Henny. Thank you so much. We must make tracks quite soon.'

Marijke bustled back into the kitchen and reappeared with tea and a plate of juicy cookies of her own making. They went well with another glass of liqueur.

He adores her, thought Henny, as Sylvia led Stan out to the car. And I don't wonder. Sylvia put out her hand to be shaken. She was quite warm-hearted enough not to be a kisser. 'Thank you. It's been a lovely day. I've enjoyed myself so much. I hope you'll return the compliment and come to us. Stan would love it, I know. He talks about you often. He really misses you. I don't know much about advertising, I keep out of it. But I know he thinks you're a genius.'

Henny laughed and smiled and waved, her arm through Lucy's as Stan wound down the window by the passenger seat and waved back. Henny watched as Sylvia adjusted the seat, fixed the driving mirror, checked her own and Stan's seat-belts. With a cheerful toot on the horn, they were at last off. 'What a lovely couple,' said Henny to Jack, as they turned back into their house. 'She's great, isn't she?'

'Stan would be lost without her.' Jack put his arm round Henny and kissed her in front of his mother and father. 'And I'd be lost without you, my darling. Well done, a great day.'

'If you don't kind,' said Marijke, 'I would like to go to my room now, for a little rest.' She departed upstairs and closed her bedroom door as loudly as she could. From the way she observed Jack looking at Henny, it was high time they should be alone for an hour or two. And please God, to make a baby.

'Will you take me for a ride in your car?' asked Jack.

'But you've been in my car. I take you to the station.'

'I'm always too distracted to notice it. But it's an interesting car.'

'You can have a go, if you want to,' said Henny.

'Don't be silly. I'm about eight million over the limit. And you've hardly drunk a thing. I need some exercise. Take me down to the river and let's go for a walk.'

They didn't walk very far. Henny wondered if Jack wanted to make love outdoors, which happened to be something, between their London life and his commuting life, that they had never done. Jack did, indeed, sit on the bank of the river and put his arms round her. 'There's something I want to talk to you about,' he said.

For a moment, Henny thought she was perhaps about to hear that her husband had taken a mistress. If, she thought, it is Glenda, I will be very annoyed indeed. 'So,' she said cautiously, 'what is it?'

'I'm thinking of changing jobs.'

'Is that all?'

'It's a bit risky. That's the thing. It's a new agency. Sanders and Sanders.'

'Never heard of them.'

'It's a bit risky. Sorry, I just said that, didn't I? It's just that I'm, well, bored with WTS.'

'Don't blame you.' Henny laid her head on Jack's shoulder

and said not one word about all she knew of Kevin Preston-Jackson. 'Go for it,' she said and kissed his neck.

15

Lucy knew perfectly well that Cecilia was gradually failing. But she detested it when Mrs Phillips, on occasions when she couldn't avoid coming face to face with the woman, bandied such phrases as 'Going downhill', 'There comes a time when curing gives way to caring' and, with an impertinent assumption of knowing Lucy's mind better than Lucy did herself, announcing 'Of course you don't want to lose her. And she could go on a long time, properly sheltered.'

Betty Boxendale said to her friend Bobby, 'I'll have to go and see my mother.'

Bobby looked up, worm-pill in hand. 'Oh dear. Is she ill?'

'No. But I haven't been there since Christmas. And Mrs Phillips gave me a hint. She's so good. Marvellous, really. She rings me if she thinks there's anything to worry about. And she's just rung, as a matter of fact.'

'But if your mother's not actually ill . . . I mean, there's the show at Swindon next week. And you know we're putting the pup into the novice class.'

'Oh, I won't go until after that.' The pup, owing to judicial prejudice, only got Reserve at Swindon. As soon as she could put her indignation behind her, Betty telephoned Mrs Phillips and announced her impending arrival, together with a full explanation of where the pup should have come – second place at the very least.

'I don't know,' said Mrs Phillips in her being-tactful voice, 'if you were thinking of bringing the dogs. But, and you know I never interfere, it might be better not. Your mother really isn't up to it.'

Well at least, thought Maxine, opening the door to Miss Boxendale, she hasn't brought those blooming dogs with her.

Actually Betty, in Maxine's opinion, wasn't such a bad old stick, specially for a teacher. Anyway, she'd retired. Maxine regarded retired teachers as some regard old lags gone straight at last. The only thing she really had against Betty was that she was too thick by half with that Mrs Phillips.

'Maxine does her best,' said Mrs Phillips to Betty while Maxine was trying to dust round the pair of them.

'Maxine,' said Cecilia pointedly, 'keeps everything clean and tidy and is all the help I need.' Maxine did not miss the significant look heavily directed at Betty by Mrs Phillips. If Mrs Phillips chose to assume that domestics were deaf, that was her problem.

Replacing the Copenhagen bird, with ostentatious care, in its exact place, Maxine put her duster in her pocket. 'Now. Would you like to come out round the garden, Mrs Boxendale?' she asked.

Unable to prevent this dangerous exercise, Mrs Phillips had to content herself with the advice, 'Mind you don't fall, dear.'

'She won't.' If looks were being exchanged, Maxine was as good at that game as anybody and Mrs Phillips received one that dared her to push her luck an inch further.

Out in the garden, Cecilia, her arm through Maxine's – another nice thing about Maxine was that she didn't grab one by the arm from behind and tip one over – managed to get breath enough to say, 'Thank you, Maxine. That showed her.'

Betty was in the house for four days, during which Mrs Phillips paid constant visits. It was cat and mouse for Maxine. But for all her assiduous stalking, it was impossible to drive a wedge between Betty and the predator. On the third day, she sought out Henny. 'What does power of attorney mean?' she asked abruptly.

'I haven't the faintest idea. Why do you want to know?'

'Because I was listening. It's something Mrs Boxendale has signed. It must be legal. See, Mr Dormer came to the house this morning. Mrs Phillips was there, and she'd brought Mrs Merritt. He'd brought these papers and he was explaining them to Betty.'

'But surely if my father-in-law was there it must have been business of Mrs Boxendale's? He's her solicitor.'

'I know. But they didn't, none of them, seem to tell her anything. Just got her to sign the paper. And then Mrs Merritt signed it.'

'We'd best get hold of Lucy,' said Henny.

'Good idea. Hadn't thought of that. Lady Lucy, she'll know what it's about, won't she?'

Henny picked up the telephone. 'Lucy? Are you busy, or could you pop down to my house? I've got Maxine here.'

'I hope nothing's wrong with Cecilia? She's not ill?'

'No. But it *is* about her.'

'I'll be right there.'

Lucy arrived to find Henny openly smoking a cigarette. 'I could do with one myself,' said Maxine.

'No you don't,' said Henny. 'Don't you start. Just look on me as a bad example but I don't care at the moment. I'll open all the windows before Jack gets home. Or maybe I won't. Lucy, thanks for coming. Do you know anything about a thing called a power of attorney?'

'Yes, I do. My father had to give power of attorney when he went gaga. There wasn't any money. That had all galloped off on horseback. And the wine merchants hadn't done too badly, either. So, no money but a lot of property. Full cellars and no central heating as I remember only too well! Anyway, yes, there was this power of attorney but I can't for the life of me remember whether the idea was to stop him from selling it all or to make him sell it to the highest bidder. My husband handled it, I know that. And he did it very well. Daddy went into a nursing home. He loved it, he'd never been so comfortable in his life. And the nurses took his bets. But that was Ireland.'

Maxine was fascinated by this tale of high life. 'What about her ladyship? Did she like the nursing home?'

Lucy pulled herself back to the present. 'She never got there. She died the day the castle was sold.'

'But,' said Henny, 'this power of attorney. With Cecilia, I mean.'

'With my father, it was given to my brother. He was the heir.'

Maxine chipped in. 'I think it's Betty has got it. I didn't

understand what they were on about so I listened as hard as I could. I wish I'd got a look at it, though.'

'That's something I can find out. I'll ask Peter about it. I'll go now. Give me a cup of coffee, Henny, will you? I need my wits about me.'

'Shall I come with you?' asked Henny.

'No. I'll go.'

'Coo,' said Maxine as Lucy departed. 'Must be serious. She's that sort of lady she'd never go and interrupt her husband while he's at work. You sure I can't have a cigarette?'

'Absolutely. You get back down there to Mrs Boxendale. Give her a glass of sherry.'

'You don't have to tell me,' said Maxine as she departed.

Peter Dormer's receptionist announced Lady Lucy. One look told her that her employer's wife was not to be fobbed off. 'Funny,' she said to the other girl, as Lady Lucy swept up the curved staircase. 'She never comes here, not usually. Hope nothing's wrong.'

'I fancy tuna-fish salad sandwich for my lunch,' said the other girl. 'Your turn to get it.'

'What a pleasant surprise,' said Peter.

Lucy looked round the large, pleasant room that was Peter's office. Thank goodness he'd wanted those chairs of Mummy's. They looked well here and the price of sitting in discomfort was a small one to pay, for clients who expected to deal with a solicitor of taste. 'I'm sorry,' she said, 'to disturb you when you are busy. But it is something important.'

Peter wrinkled his brow. Had he forgotten Lucy's birthday, or was it their wedding anniversary? He glanced at his diary to see if his lunch engagement could be put off. 'So tell me,' he smiled. 'What is it?'

'It's about Cecilia.'

'Oh. Yes.' In a trice, Peter reverted to his solicitoring manner. Lucy watched him looking as though he had to call for a file before he could quite remember who Cecilia was. 'You were there, this morning. Remember?'

'Oh yes.'

'The power of attorney. I take it you have given Betty Boxendale power of attorney?'

'That is correct. There's nothing to sound so upset about. I assure you, I know what I am doing.'

'But does Cecilia?'

'Don't you see, my dear? That's why we've done it. Cecilia doesn't know much, nowadays. I know how fond you are of her but the fact of the matter is that she can't handle her own affairs any longer. She is ninety-five, you know.'

'Yes,' said Lucy evenly, 'I do know that. But what affairs has she got to handle, except living out her life in peace?'

'Precisely. That is what we are trying to help her to do.'

'In The Elms. That's what Mrs Phillips is planning. At £500 a week.'

'Mrs Phillips isn't "planning", as you put it, anything. I have merely arranged for the daughter to have power of attorney.'

'Have you any idea of the influence Mrs Phillips has on Betty?'

'You're being fanciful. And, in any case, what is wrong with The Elms? Cecilia,' he added with unfortunate incaution, 'is quite well off.'

'Hah,' said Lucy.

'And also,' added Peter, 'not at all well.'

'How do you know that?'

'I play golf with Phillips. He is, after all, Cecilia's physician. He told me, in confidence, that he's fairly sure she has already had a couple of small strokes.'

'He got that from *her*, I presume.'

'You mean Kathleen Phillips, do you? You may not like her. I know you don't. But she has been very good to Cecilia and very concerned for her.'

'Hah,' said Lucy again. 'And I take it Mr Merritt the bank manager also plays golf. And he's clinging on to his job and you're a good customer and Cecilia is quite well off. Dr Phillips the Physician, Mrs Phillips the Physician's Wife. Mr Merritt the Manager, and so on. Happy Families.'

'You've lost me,' said Peter.

'Never mind,' said Lucy wearily. 'She's signed the damn thing, hasn't she?'

'Yes. Would you like a cup of coffee? Or tea? I can get them to make one.'

'No. I'll go home now. I'm sure you have a lunch appointment.'

'I could break it.'

'No thank you.'

Lucy drove herself home and went to the shed which had once been the home of Heraclitus. She sat on the floor and wept.

During the afternoon, Henny received a telephone call from Stan Howard. 'Henny? Listen, girl, I need you.'

'What's up, Stan?'

'That bloke who replaced you. Replaced, there's a joke. Anyway, he's left. Thank God. I was trying to work out how I could fire him. Listen, sweetheart, I know I'm being selfish, but I really need you. Could you even give me a couple of days a week?'

'I'll think about it. I really will.'

'If you're worrying about being back in the same agency with Jack . . .'

'I'm not. Not in the least. He's leaving. I don't know whether you knew that?'

'Heavens. The one thing I was afraid of was that you didn't know. He's going to Sanders and Sanders.'

'He told me. Just after you and Sylvia came to lunch.'

'So will you do it? Even a couple of days a week would help me.'

'That's no way to do it, Stan, and you know it. If I'm going to make any sort of a fist of it, I'll have to come back full time. I'll talk it over with Jack and let you know. And there are other considerations, as well.' Such, she thought after she had rung off, as how the hell are we going to save Cecilia? She'd rather be in her grave than in The Elms.

16

Cecilia Boxendale awoke on the morning of 31 July and lay still in her bed, that last warm moment before the day had to be faced. If she sat up, she could just see the leaves on the cherry tree, already turning bronze now that the blossom had long gone. The blackbird also had long ago launched her children. Her nest was empty.

'There isn't a chestnut tree in this garden,' she said to Maxine. Maxine had forbidden her to get out of bed until she arrived, with tea and toast.

'Isn't there? Sit up a bit, will you, please, Mrs Boxendale.' Maxine thrust her quiet hand under the bedclothes. A bit damp but not too bad. Mrs Boxendale needn't know. That Mrs Phillips, with her 'We can get you some incontinence knickers.' The cheek of it. 'Tell me about chestnut trees,' she said, watching carefully as Mrs Boxendale took her cup of tea.

'There were two chestnut trees. At home. I used to climb up and get conkers.'

'Fancy! I didn't know girls did things like that, in your days. I thought you would've worn long skirts.'

'We did. And corsets. But I didn't need the corsets. That was one advantage of being tall and thin. I was quite a tomboy.'

Maxine chuckled 'I'll bet you were!'

'You asked me about the chestnut tree. It was the chestnut leaves that turned brown first.' She continued, as Maxine had intended her to: 'How fast the year goes by. Funny thing about old age; the days get longer and the years get shorter.'

'You eat your toast while it's warm. It's nice and buttery. I'm going down to tidy up and then I'll help you get dressed. I expect Henny'll be in later.'

Cecilia ate her toast to please Maxine and actually enjoyed

it. Crisp little strips with the crusts cut off and enough butter to give Mrs Phillips a fit. She could hear Maxine downstairs, driving the vacuum cleaner along the passage like a racing car. So what if she banged the paintwork, as Mrs Phillips never hesitated to point out. In a half-doze she murmured, 'You know, God, I don't often get in touch. Too much church when I was a girl, really. But I'm very thankful. I don't know what I'd do without my friends. Lucy, Maxine, dear Dot Blunt. And Henny, though I worry about her.'

Maxine came up and helped her into her clothes. Maxine liked to see Mrs Boxendale nicely dressed. To that end, she did a lot of rinsing and ironing. Mrs Boxendale, in Maxine's opinion, was best off in a clean blouse and a cardie and a pair of trousers so's she wouldn't get cold. Maxine had no time for the button-through frocks they put old people into. 'They' represented everything Maxine most disliked.

She brought Mrs Boxendale downstairs and saw her into her chair. Henny came in just at the right moment, so she could leave Mrs Boxendale comfortable and tidy up in the kitchen.

After a short silence, Henny said in a rush, 'There's something I want to talk to you about.'

Cecilia very much hoped she was not about to hear the secrets of the marriage bed. People talked about sex so much these days; they even had, she understood, therapists for it and those ridiculous counsellors. It had taken her a time to learn that counsellor wasn't spelt councillor, which at least cleared up a worrying misapprehension. In her long life in Tiddingfold, she had been coerced into attending exceedingly tedious meetings of the Borough Council. Those grey, pompous men, oh dear, imagine them taking it upon themselves to teach people how to make love!

'Jack is changing jobs. He's leaving WTS, where I also used to work, you know. He's going to a firm called Sanders and Sanders, as managing director.'

'That sounds all right.'

'It could be. It's a new firm, not established yet. So it's a bit of a risk. I don't mind that. I want him to do it, as a matter of fact.'

'So. What is the problem?'

'My old boss, Stan Howard, wants me to go back and work for him again.'

'So. Are you going to do it?'

'I can't quite decide. Jack is very happy with our home here. And so am I, in a lot of ways. Lucy. And you. And Maxine and Dot. But I have to tell you that when Stan asked me if I'd like to come back, I just felt the most tremendous wave of excitement. But you see, I know it's what *I* want. What about Jack? Anyone can see he loves to be the breadwinner. I can see that myself. Ever since we were married. Would I be undermining him?'

'I don't know about that. But if you say his new venture has an element of risk, wouldn't he think it a good idea to have your salary, just in case?'

'It would make sense, yes. But is sense always the best thing?'

Cecilia was getting tired and sherry-minded. 'You'd better ask him. If you're talking of undermining, I should think not talking to him about what's on your mind would be about the worst thing you could do.'

Henny looked with admiration at Cecilia. It was sometimes hard to remember she was ninety-five. That she was perfectly capable of listening and understanding, Henny had long taken for granted. But that she could so readily comprehend Henny's way of life, a way of life that had been denied her in her own long-ago youth, was remarkable. And to think that, behind her back, a plot was afoot to incarcerate her in The Elms.

She fetched the Amontillado.

The days of August drifted by, one slipping into another. 'We haven't seen much of Mrs Phillips lately,' said Cecilia one day, as Dot was pouring out the sherry.

'Good thing too,' said Maxine.

It was on a Monday afternoon, almost at the end of the month, that the blow fell. Lucy got an agitated telephone call. It was Dot Blunt, not very coherent. 'Could you come? I'm sorry to bother you. I told Maxine I was going to phone you and she said yes, I'd better, she said. It's that Power thing, she said. I didn't know what she was talking about but she said it must be through that and I didn't know what to do so she said get you.'

'Dot, dear, what exactly has happened?'

'I'm sorry. I was that upset I've had a couple of sherries. But I know what I'm saying. We had a phone call. From an estate agent. I answered, you see, and they said was I Miss Boxendale and I said you must mean Mrs Boxendale and like a fool I put her on the line, what a fool, oh dear. She looks terrible. I thought she was going to faint. All she could say was "My house. Selling my house." So I got back on the phone myself and yes, bold as brass, the man said he wanted to send someone round this afternoon, to view. So I said no, Mrs Boxendale is not well and I rang off.'

'I'll come at once.'

'I've given her a drop of brandy, I hope that was all right. She was blue.'

Probably all wrong, thought Lucy, jumping into the car. But so what? Maxine opened the front door of Cecilia's house. Lucy ran in and held Cecilia's hand, tightly. 'Would you like to go to bed?' she asked.

'No, I would not,' said Cecilia. But she did allow Maxine to put her into her big armchair.

'Racing time,' said Maxine, putting on the TV good and loud. It was cartoons, but the racket allowed Lucy a moment to ring the estate agent's and tell them to send no one, for the time being. They said they were sorry but these were definitely Miss Boxendale's instructions.

'Very well. I'll speak to Miss Boxendale. But please do nothing at present.'

'She may miss a sale. The market's dreadful but we've got someone definitely interested. We've done well, there. Go down to winter and it'll be a different story.'

Dot was weeping in the kitchen. Cecilia's was not the only throat down which a drop of medicinal brandy had been poured. Lucy's one wish was to get hold of Betty Boxendale and get to the bottom of the whole business. But if she telephoned from here, Cecilia, who was looking terrible but had not been stricken deaf, would hear every word. Please God, let Henny be at home. Luckily, she was.

Lucy explained as quickly as she could, adding, 'and poor dear Dot has not only poured brandy down Cecilia's throat but I'm very much afraid she's crocked herself as well. Maxine's there, thank God.'

'I'll go straight along and see what I can do, while you try and get Betty, damn her.'

Betty, called away in the middle of french-chalking a show-dog, was mildly surprised to hear from Lucy Dormer in the middle of the afternoon.

Lucy, before dialling, had taken several deep breaths, so as to sound calm. Yes, she learnt, it was quite true. The house was on the market. 'You see,' said Betty, 'we thought it best. It's going to be quite expensive for her to live at The Elms. Though of course, Mrs Phillips is frightfully helpful. She's going to charge £20 a week less than the usual rate. For long term, she says. She's so good.'

Long term, thought Lucy grimly. I wouldn't give much hope of Cecilia surviving long term at The Elms, with its 'cheery' day-room, chairs backed in a line against the wall, old heads drooping, slippered feet dangling. She'd go off her head and I can't see Mrs Phillips liking *that*. Into the geriatric psycho ward, or whatever they call it. The bitch. 'But,' she said evenly, 'I thought we had all agreed that The Elms was not a good idea for your mother.'

'Did we? Really, I think you've got it all wrong about The Elms. It's lovely. Lovely garden. What we thought, Mrs Phillips and I, is that we'll just suggest she goes in for a week or two, maybe while Maxine has a holiday. And then she'll settle in and love it.'

'And do you really believe she'll swallow that "week or two" story? She's not half-witted. And she's just discovered you've put the house on the market.'

'Oh dear. I do hope she's not upset. I'm only trying to do what's best for her. Do you think I ought to come down? It's frightfully difficult to get away just now. But if you think I ought to, I'll come.'

'Oh no, I don't think that's necessary.' Nor advisable, thought Lucy, unless you wish me to strangle you with my bare hands.

144

'Oh dear. You sound annoyed. It's so difficult to do the right thing.'

'Yes,' said Lucy. 'It is, isn't it? Very difficult.'

'What? What did you say? Down, Jasper, sit. Si–it, si–it. Sorry, but you have to make them sit when you tell them to. Look, I'll be down as soon as I can. By the way, the nice thing about The Elms is that they let them take in one or two bits of their own as long as they're small. That's so thoughtful, isn't it?'

'Very. Goodbye, Betty.' Lucy rang off.

She went back to Cecilia's house. Dot Blunt emerged from the kitchen, drunkenly upright on her dainty ankles. She went to Cecilia's chair and, just managing to lean without falling, said, 'Mrs Boxendale, everything will be quite all right.'

'I'm sure it will,' said Cecilia.

'I'll go now,' said Dot, with dignity. 'See you tomorrow?'

'I'll run you home,' said Henny.

'Not at all. The walk will do me good.' Dot know she was in no fit state to face Major Blunt just yet.

'Come and have a cup of tea, in my house,' said Henny.

Dot drank her tea. 'This is enough to give her a stroke,' she said, wishing the tea were brandy but accepting that Henny knew best.

Lucy and Maxine at last persuaded Cecilia up to bed. 'It's broad daylight,' complained Cecilia. 'I can hear them playing tennis.'

'Just a rest,' said Maxine. 'Half an hour. Take you round the garden later, promise. I'm just going downstairs to tidy up.'

Lucy followed her down, 'Tennis? There's no tennis court within a mile.'

'They had a tennis court at her home. She's told me, she hated to go to bed on summer evenings when she was a child. She used to hear the grown-ups playing tennis. She wanders a bit, sometimes.' More than a bit, but Maxine usually kept quiet on that score. 'If you'd go up and chat to her she'll soon be all right.'

Lucy sat by the bed. Eventually, Cecilia drifted into sleep. Lucy kissed her. Her legs ached as she dragged herself downstairs.

Maxine was running water into the kitchen sink. 'Phew. Poor old lady. Diarrhoea and all. This cushion. Past praying for. Dustbin, that's where I'm putting it. Can they really sell her house, Lady Lucy?'

'They can,' said Lucy. 'That's what power of attorney is all about.'

'Blooming liberty.'

'It's what Betty thinks best. It's her business, not ours. The Elms is well thought of. I suppose we've got to look at it that way.'

'I'd sooner drop down dead. My grandpa did. Heart attack and gone. Look, Lady Lucy, you go home. There's nothing more you can do. I'll settle her.'

Lucy drove home. It was getting late and she made a vague search round the freezer to see what she could dig out for Peter's dinner. Angry as she was that it was he who had perpetrated this disaster, it could never have entered her head not to make dinner for him. She had no appetite herself and no desire to drink. She envied Dot Blunt her escape route. She had a splitting headache.

She was not given to headaches. Even the death of Heraclitus had not brought on a headache. All she had had to do, on that sad day, was to cradle the tortoise in her arms and bid him goodbye.

Now what did one take for headaches? Aspirin. There must be some aspirin in the bathroom cabinet. She searched. Half-used tubes of ointments, bottles of pills shoved to the back. Something Peter had been supposed to take when his heart missed a beat. Sleeping pills. She examined the unopened bottle. It had her name on it. Lady Dormer. 'I'm not Lady Dormer,' she thought vaguely, turning the bottle in her hands and reading the instructions: ' "One to be taken at night . . ." I'm Lady Lucy Dormer, not that it matters. Anyway, what is this?' The headache seemed to recede as she remembered a day, two, or was it three years ago, when she had ventured to go to Dr Phillips. It came back. She had not been feeling very well.

'Sleep? How do you sleep?'

'Oh,' she had said vaguely. 'I don't need much sleep.'

Dr Phillips had ushered her out with a prescription. With a

feeling that she had been wasting his time, Lucy had had the prescription filled and then put it in the back of the bathroom cabinet. She didn't mind not sleeping.

The day they could no longer prevent the estate agent from showing his buyers the house was a nightmare. Henny tried to get Cecilia out of the way with an invitation to lunch. But Cecilia was only just well enough to get downstairs, and that with breathless difficulty.

Lucy tried to protect Cecilia but the couple, nice sixty-year-olds, were determined to be gracious. 'We love your house, Mrs Boxendale. I'm sure you'll be sorry to leave it. Where are you going?'

'Nowhere,' snapped Cecilia. Lucy got rid of them as fast as she could.

By the time Lucy and Maxine got her up to bed, Cecilia's hands were trembling and one leg was dragging ominously. Her face looked somehow floppy. The usually resilient Maxine was frightened. 'Do you think we ought to get the doctor?' she asked.

'She looks better, now she's in bed. One of us ought to stay the night.'

'You're knackered. I'll stay.'

'No. You're exhausted too.' Lucy was not about to insult Maxine, but she decided firmly that what the night might bring was too much for a sixteen-year old. 'I'll get Henny. That's the best idea. Jack's so fond of Mrs Boxendale he'll quite understand.'

Henny came at once and Lucy went home. 'I'll be with you first thing,' she said.

To Henny's surprise, it was almost midday before Lucy appeared, looking dreadful. 'I'm so sorry. I couldn't sleep, so I took a pill. I've never taken one in my life before. It knocked me out.'

'Lucy darling. We can't go on like this. The fact of the matter is, she's bedridden. I don't honestly think, and neither does Maxine, she'll ever get up again. And she really is incontinent. Blasted Mrs Phillips is right about that. It's only due to Maxine that she doesn't know it herself. We really ought to get the doctor.'

Lucy found herself weeping. 'You know what that means.'

'I do. But let's face it, the house is sold. I hate it as much as you do. I know it's worse for you, you've known her so much longer.'

'You're right. I know you are. But she talks perfectly clearly. Surely it can't have been a stroke? Look, I'll stay with her tonight, and tomorrow, I promise you, we'll get the doctor.'

'All right then. You go home and get some rest and come back later.'

Far from resting, Lucy wandered about the empty house all afternoon. She went out to Heraclitus's shed. She still hadn't brought herself to throw his box away. She heard the telephone ring and hurried back indoors. It was Penelope. The baby had colic and Nanny was worse than useless. Lucy remembered how good Cecilia had been with Jack and his repulsive nappies, all those years ago, made some helpful noises, quite cheered Penelope up and rang off.

She hardly knew what she was doing, as she went to the medicine cupboard. It was as though somebody other than herself took the bottle of sleeping pills down to the kitchen and, tipping the contents out on to the table, crushed them up. She removed the label from the bottle, tore it up and threw the bottle into the dustbin. Then she put the crushed pills into a silver snuff box which commemorated the Crimean and Boer Wars, the property of her late grandfather, the Earl before her own father. It was a pretty box, the sort of artefact anyone might have on a table, even a bedside table. She then sat quite still for half an hour.

'No sponge cake this afternoon?' asked Maxine, as Mrs Boxendale waved away the tray she had taken up. 'Mrs Blunt made it for you, it's lovely and fresh.'

'Never you mind,' said Dot, who had followed Maxine into the bedroom. 'It'll keep till tomorrow. And Maxine'll have a slice, won't you, Maxine?'

'Want to try and come downstairs? In your dressing gown?' asked Maxine, knowing it was impossible.

'No thank you, my dear. I'm very comfortable here. You've put on the nice sheets, haven't you? I'll just lie and look out at the garden. Seems very dark. Is it night already?' It was broad daylight. 'We've done a lot together, haven't we Maxine?'

Dot Blunt stood by the window. 'Would you like a sherry?' Cecilia invited.

'No thank you. I did very well at lunchtime. Can you hear the birds?'

Cecilia nodded.

'I'll have to cut that grass,' said Maxine. 'It'll need at least one more cut before winter.' She was trying to kid Mrs Boxendale that winter would see her still in her own home.

A little later, Henny came in. 'It's a lovely day, so sunny.' Dot Blunt looked at her and shook her head.

Maxine went over to the bed. 'We're going to have to trim your hair. It's ever such a mess.'

'If I was young again,' said Mrs Boxendale, 'I'd have my hair done just like yours, Maxine. It's very jolly. I like the colours.'

'Do you? Really?'

'Really.'

'It's only a rinse. Washes out, if you don't like what you've done.' Her little face was white, of itself, not of one of her makeups. 'Lady Lucy's coming in tonight. I'm off. Got to give the kids their tea, Mum's going out. See ya. God bless.' She bent down, kissed Mrs Boxendale and hurried out of the room and out of the house.

There was a boyfriend waiting for her outside. 'Want to go to the pictures? I got a car.'

'Oh, piss off,' said Maxine. Funny girl, he thought. She's crying.

Dot Blunt stayed on until Lucy arrived. At home, she was restless all evening, couldn't seem to settle. 'You haven't sat still for two minutes,' said the Major. 'What's the matter with you?'

'I'm sorry, dear.'

'You worried about the old lady? I'll run you up there after dinner, if you like. Put your mind at rest.'

Dot gazed at the Major, tears filling her eyes. It was the first sweet thing she could remember him saying since she'd produced a son. 'That's ever so kind of you. But Lady Lucy's with her. She'll see her into bed. I'm just being silly. But thank you ever so much.'

The Major felt so pleased with himself that he offered Dot a crème de menthe when he got his own post-prandial brandy.

Lucy wondered if Henny would ever go. The evening dragged on.

'You sure you'll be all right alone?' asked Henny.

'Perfectly.' Lucy sat on. The room grew dark.

'The house has been sold, hasn't it?' asked Cecilia.

'No,' lied Lucy. 'The sale fell through. That often happens, the people who wanted it were let down on the sale of their own house.'

'So I can stay here?'

'For ever.'

'I like it when you're with me, Lucy. I'm not afraid of anything, when you're here. I'd like to get up and go to the lavatory.'

Lucy helped her as she struggled out of bed, her long legs trailing ridiculously. It was far too late, the all too familiar odour of urine was already evident. But Lucy helped her to the bathroom and waited, while she drooped on the seat helplessly, the poor old bladder already emptied. Once back in bed, she seemed to doze. Within two minutes, she woke, alarmed. 'It's all right,' said Lucy, 'I'm here.'

'Oh Lucy, I am at home, aren't I?'

'Yes. You're at home.'

'I fell off my bicycle.'

'Did you? When?'

'Just now, of course. Pulled my shoulder. It aches. Hope it'll be all right for the wedding. I'd look an awful fool, going up the aisle with my arm in a sling. My dress is cream. Mother says plain white is too trying for a bride almost thirty. Mother can be very cruel.'

Lucy listened to the dreadful logic of the wandering mind. Now, she must forget the world outside this bedroom. No one existed except her and Cecilia.

'Tell me about the cream dress, Cecilia. I'm sure you looked lovely. You're so tall and slim.'

Cecilia sighed. 'Slim? Skinny, my father always said. And my nose.' Briskly, she raised her head. 'It was a long time ago, though. What am I talking about?'

'You didn't have any tea,' said Lucy. 'Now, what I want you to do, just to please me, is let me make you a hot drink. Will you?'

'All right. Don't like milk much. But if you say so.'

'I'll put a drop of brandy in it.'

'That's more like it. Dot. Dot gets rather tiddly, but I like her. Reginald used to drink brandy but he never offered me any. Dot Blunt did.'

Henny came in next morning, well before Maxine's usual hour of arrival. She found Lucy asleep with her head on Cecilia's bed and Cecilia's cold hand in hers. She washed Cecilia's face, hoping she was doing it as well as her mother Marijke would have done. She telephoned Dr Phillips, because that must be done. But, smelling brandy, she opened Cecilia's dead mouth and wiped it out with a soapy flannel.

Dot and Maxine wept. Dot put her arm round Lucy and made her go downstairs. 'Maxine and I will straighten up. Now, what's this? I never saw this silver box before; this on her bedside table. There's nothing in it. I wonder what it's meant for?'

'I expect it's something Lady Lucy brought her,' said Maxine, piling up the last of the damp sheets she would never again secrete for Mrs Boxendale. 'She's like that. She'd always think of some little thing to please Mrs Boxendale.' The box looked a bit dusty, or powdery, inside. A good rub round with the duster and a bit of silver polish would put that right.

There was no inquest.

All Tiddingfold attended the funeral. 'I am the resurrection and the life, saith the Lord,' intoned the vicar as the coffin was borne into the church. Lady Lucy had insisted he use the old form of words.

Marijke came down to help Henny prepare the wake. Whatever the Tiddingfolders might think about the vulgarity of goulash, potato pancakes, pickled cucumbers and what looked like a birthday cake, they found, as they wielded their forks in a dainty manner, that there's nothing like a funeral for giving an appetite.

Lucy had asked Marijke to stay at her house for the night. Marijke, realising that she was wanted, accepted the invitation. So, after the long day was over, Henny and Jack went up to bed by themselves. Jack wept for his old friend.

'Don't,' said Henny.

'I'm sorry. It's unmanly, isn't it?'

'No it's not. I just mean don't be sad. Be thankful she died in time.'

'Do you know how much I love you?' asked Jack.

'Yes, I do. And I would be lost without you. Jack, I want to go back to work.'

'Are you not happy here?'

'Very happy. I wouldn't part with our little house for any-thing. But Stan has asked me to work again. And I want to do it. Funnily enough, I talked to Cecilia about it shortly before she died. She thought it was a good idea.'

'Why? Because I'm taking such a risk, going to Sanders and Sanders?'

'Not really. I'm not that worried about risks. It's just that it is what I want to do. We could use the flat on weekdays and come down here every weekend.'

In a while, they both slept.

The news soon got round Tiddingfold. 'I always knew,' sniffed Mrs Phillips, 'that she didn't really belong here.'

'Poor Henny,' said Penelope, 'I did try to help her. Oh well, I suppose she thinks going back to work makes up for not having a baby.'

Betty Boxendale gave Mrs Phillips a cheque for £1,000, for The Elms. 'Only £1,000,' sniffed Mrs Merritt. 'That's not very much. After you'd been so kind. Have you heard?' she con-tinued. 'Jack and Henny are selling up.'

'Yes,' said Mrs Phillips charitably. 'Getting divorced, of course. I saw it coming. She never fitted in, in Tiddingfold.'

'Come on, sweetheart, time for dinner. Where shall we go?' asked Jack, the first night back in the flat.

'I didn't have time to shop,' said Henny.

'I know that.'

'But I can cook, now,' said Henny.

'And so you shall, at weekends. Let's go and eat and have an early night. You'll want your wits about you tomorrow. I bet Stan's loaded you with work.'

After dinner, they strolled up Long Acre, arm in arm. 'I've got to admit,' said Jack, 'that it's a lot nicer getting home without that bloody journey.'

'So you don't mind what I'm doing?'

'Come to bed.'

'Goodness,' said Henny later. 'You're very energetic.'

'You,' said Stan next morning, 'have got a smile on your face like the cat that's swallowed the cream.'

'So give me the Vara Cars script and mind your own business,' said Henny austerely.

'OK,' said Stan. 'But you've been up to no good, haven't you?'

'What *do* you mean, Stan?' asked Henny sweetly.

'Getting pregnant, I wouldn't be surprised.'

'How you do go about getting pregnant! I've been off the pill for almost a year and I haven't got pregnant yet.'

'Oh well, enjoy yourself then. But I'm not starting a crèche, I'll tell you that. And I don't approve of working mothers.'

'You can approve or not as you like. What's wrong with me?'

'Your mother is a saint,' said Stan.

'And my mother went straight back to the jam factory after I was born. So working mothers can't be such a bad thing. I used to be left with a neighbour, she was lovely and I called her Aunty. Ma hadn't got any relations alive and whether my father had or not, I don't know. I spent the first five years of my life believing people called Aunty had black faces and cuddled you a lot. So kindly mind your own business and let me get on with some work.'

'And then go home and bonk.'

'You put it so elegantly.'

At the weekend, Henny and Jack went down to Tiddingfold.

Mrs Phillips had noted that both their cars were parked in the forecourt of the local garage, which annoyed her, conflicting as it did with her decision that divorce was imminent.

Lucy picked them up at Ashden station, gave them supper at Alexandra Lodge and, afterwards, dropped them off at Mulberry Cottage.

It was a cold night. 'We'll have to arrange for someone to come in and turn on the heating,' said Henny, shivering. 'Poor little house, it doesn't like being empty.'

'How about a cup of tea before bed?' asked Jack. They drank their tea in the kitchen. Jack yawned sleepily.

Henny stretched. 'I'm just going outside for a breath of air. Don't lock me out!'

'All right. Don't be long.'

'I won't.' She closed the front door quietly and went the few steps up the high street, to say a last goodnight to Mrs Boxendale.

The new owners of Cecilia's house had cleared the straggle of roses out of the little front garden, which was now smartly paved. Hanging baskets of flowers that didn't match colour with colour dangled either side of the front door, above which an imitation carriage lamp sent out a startling beam of yellow light. The swags of curtains which fussily disfigured the window of the sitting-room would have caused Cecilia to snort with contempt.

So that was all over. Cecilia was gone. Henny turned back to her own house. It crossed her mind that she might ask Ma if she would like to give up her flat and come down to live there. But she rapidly dismissed the idea. People must live the way they needed to live.

But she realised that she had come to love Mulberry Cottage. She couldn't pretend she was treating it as other than a weekend cottage, but it deserved better than to spend its weekdays locked and cold. She sat in the dark on the low front garden wall. 'Nice little garden to handle when we're old,' she said to it.

She went in and locked the door behind her. Jack was still awake. 'You've been up to Cecilia's house, haven't you?' he said. 'You mustn't be sad about her.'

'I'm not. It's just that I was thinking, all that time I spent with her, somehow there's more of me here than I'd realised. I can't bear to neglect our house.'

'No need. Get someone to come in two or three times a week and see to it.'

'Yes, but who?'

'I should have thought it was obvious. Your little friend Maxine's out of a job now she's lost Cecilia.'

'That would be great. But oughtn't I to be encouraging her to get more education? She shouldn't waste her life.'

'And who are you to tell her what to do with her life? She doesn't tell you. Nobody tells you, I've learnt that.'

Henny laughed. 'I'll go and see her tomorrow.'

'You do that. And now for goodness sake, if you want to mind anybody's business, come to bed and mind mine.'

'I'm going to look after Mulberry Cottage,' said Maxine to Mrs Blunt, outside the shop.

'That shop,' said Dot Blunt. 'Their chickens. Hopeless. What did you say, dear?'

Maxine repeated her statement and added, 'Housekeeper, Henny said. I'm to keep house while they're in London. I hope I can do it all right.'

'Of course you can. Anyway, I can always help you if you're stuck. Nice to think they've not gone away for good. Mrs Boxendale would have liked that.'

'Yes,' said Maxine. 'They don't half overcharge for a bottle of Flash in that shop. But I've got the kitchen floor to do.'

'Never mind. When you're seventeen you'll pass your driving test and then you can go anywhere.'

They walked together up the high street. 'Come in,' said Maxine, 'and have a sherry.'

'Should I?' asked Mrs Blunt.

'Henny put me in charge.'

'All we need now,' said Mrs Blunt, 'is for Lady Lucy to drop in.'

'She will,' said Maxine. 'Give it time.'

There follows Chapter One of

FLOWERING JUDAS by **Elizabeth Palmer**

available in Arrow from June 20th. If you enjoy it,
we invite you to take up the offer at the back of
this book.

FLOWERING JUDAS
Elizabeth Palmer

Charmian Sinclair runs her own PR firm and a regular series of married lovers, one for each day of the week. Weekends are spent with Giles Hayward in Sussex. It is a rewarding way of life, but when Giles, the only bachelor in her set, falls in love with a country neighbour, Charmian realizes it can't go on for ever.

Charmian's opportunities for reflection are cut short, however, by the news that Oliver Curtis, her brother-in-law, has been brutally fired from his high-powered City job. Outraged by this, Charmian resolves to exact revenge through her own influential contacts – and discovers far more than she bargained for . . .

With wit, candour and more than a touch of brilliance, Elizabeth Palmer offers another comedy of sparkling bad manners.

Praise for previous novels by Elizabeth Palmer:

The Stainless Angel 'Beautifully executed' TODAY

Plucking the Apple 'A sharp, stylish novel of adultery' SHE

'*Old Money* seethes with possibilities . . . brisk and witty sexual episodes' THE TIMES

1

By most people's standards, Charmian Sinclair led an unconventional life. It was one that was concealed not only from her immediate family but also from others who shared it on an intimate basis, or who thought they did. Charmian believed in variety, and that to experience as much as one could in every conceivable way was the sole point of earthly existence. It was with this aim in mind that she had a series of London lovers, one for every day of the week except Friday when she went off to the country to spend the weekend with Giles Hayward.

Giles, who loathed big cities and especially capitals, lived in Sussex where he eked out a small living running his own organic garden centre and arboretum, and landscaping gardens. Theirs was a bittersweet relationship, for both, in their heart of hearts, realized it to be doomed: Giles because he knew he ultimately wanted a wife and children to share his cottage, and probably a dog as well, and this would involve a degree of rural commitment foreign to Charmian's nature; and Charmian because she liked her life as it was and was aware that with the arrangement as it stood she got as much of the country as she wanted. Any more would have been surplus to requirements. Yet the country was Giles's life, and their weekend arrangement, she recognized, could not go on for ever. All the same, without being in love with Giles, she probably loved him more than she knew and because he was her only unmarried lover felt in an odd way proprietorial where he was concerned. Eventually, said Charmian to herself, I will lose Giles, but whoever takes him had better be good because if she isn't good enough I won't let him go. Separately, then, they both took the decision to enjoy one another for as long as possible, and never speculated about their joint future. This tacit acknowledgement of evanescence clouded their relationship and at the same time gave it a poignant intensity which enhanced it, and Giles knew that, whoever else he might meet, he would never quite forget the lift

1

of his heart as Charmian stepped lightly off the train and into his arms on a Friday evening.

The other lovers were different. Charmian saw each of them on a different day of the week. Always the same day, though, otherwise confusion might have set in. So Monday was Dominic Goddard night, Tuesday was Gervase Hanson night and so on. They were all hand-picked for similar qualities, namely a talent to amuse and good looks, and all four were high-flyers, though in different professions. Charmian liked the aura of power, finding it exciting. Like a fire in a winter landscape, success drew others to it, bestowing its glamorous burnish on those privileged enough to be able to draw near. And because they were all happily married (or so they said) the other lovers evinced little curiosity as to how she conducted her life when she was not with them. That suited Charmian down to the ground. So there were dinners and lunches and opera and ballet and, since all the lovers came from different disciplines, it proved possible to compartmentalize her life successfully without embarrassing anybody in the process. Discretion was all and, because everybody knew the rules, so far it had worked.

It was the second week of June and in his garden, Giles was tending his herbaceous border, watched and occasionally unhelpfully helped by Charmian. Charmian's knowledge of horticulture was greater than it had been before she met Giles but not much. Observing her pulling up a camellia, apparently believing it to be a weed, Giles silently took it from her and heeled it back in. Unabashed, his lover smiled up at him.

'I'll never be a gardener,' said Charmian.

'No, you never will,' said Giles, kissing her on the lips. 'Why don't you leave my herbaceous borders alone and go and cut some roses for the house instead?'

Obediently she went.

For the first time ever Giles had invited a neighbour to supper while she was staying there. Whether Giles himself recognized the fact or not (and he probably did not) Charmian intuited that this heralded a change in their relationship, possibly a profound one. She found the secateurs. The day was close and dull. It was very hot, with distant thunder circling around.

The massed clouds were aubergine and there was a sluggishness in the air of the sort which is only ended by a violent electrical storm. I'd better be quick, thought Charmian, before the heavens open.

The loaded atmosphere had brought out the fragrance of the flowers. Standing among the roses, a basket on one arm, Charmian experienced a sudden feeling of peace, stability even. She cut a few of the long-stemmed variety for the one vase Giles possessed and a cluster of floribundas for the table. Some drops of rain fell, heavy and straight like stones, causing the baked earth to release its own heady smell.

With a theatrical explosion of thunder the storm broke.

There was no question of getting to the house in time and Charmian did not even consider it. Instead she let one hand fall so that the basket dangled, pushed back her long, dark hair and turned her face up to the heavy blows of the rain. Its warm assault drenched her and at the same time filled her with elation.

When Giles found her she was still there, standing stock still, face uplifted, eyes closed. She looked ecstatic. Her thin cotton dress clung to her slim body and her bare feet were spattered with wet earth. Like an Indian bride she was surrounded by heaps of rose petals which had been plucked and scattered by the sheer force of the deluge. It was an image which was to remain with him until the day he died. Without a word, he unzipped the wet dress and peeled it off her, kissing her as he did so. They made love lying on the soaked aromatic earth among the drifts of rose petals.

'Oh, this is what life in the country should be about,' murmured Charmian, enjoying herself and him, 'not weeding at all.'

Laughing and, at the same time, deeply pessimistic, he pressed her to him. 'Promise me you'll never leave me, Charmian! Please promise!'

'I'll never leave you. It is you who will leave me.'

Silencing his protest with a finger to his lips, she rose to her feet.

'You look like a bacchant,' teased Charmian.

'And you look like a nymph. The goddess of the garden!'

She slanted a smile at him. 'Would it were so!'

Separately thoughtful, they went together into the house.

Sitting opposite Karen Wyndham that evening, observing her by the light of two candles which Giles, still a student at heart and without a candlestick to his name, had pushed into the necks of a couple of defunct red wine bottles, Charmian knew without any shadow of a doubt that she was the one. Giles, of course, did not know it, and neither did Karen herself as yet, but nevertheless, there it was. Sooner than Charmian might have hoped.

Karen was not as slim as Charmian. Rather there was an elasticity about her figure and a mobility about her face which together suggested pliability without weakness. Karen would bend but she probably would not break, decided Charmian. So quite tough, in the best kind of way.

'Have you always lived in the country?' asked Charmian, refilling Karen's glass and then Giles's and lastly her own.

'Always! I wouldn't want to live anywhere else. What about you?'

Charmian imagined an AGA-ed Karen baking her own bread, wearing a long, very white apron. It was a wholesome picture.

'I'm a city girl, born and bred.' She did not elaborate, but noticed the other woman shoot a speculative glance at the back of Giles who was currently standing by the oven carving a roast chicken which was the only thing he knew how to cook. She can't work us out, thought Charmian. She feels we don't quite add up as a couple and, of course, she's right.

Into the lull which ensued, Karen said, 'We used to farm . . .'

'We?' queried Giles unexpectedly, who had appeared not to be listening to them while he concentrated on dismembering the bird.

That question told Charmian as nothing else could that, still without knowing it, Giles was drawn to this woman.

'My husband and I.' There was a short silence while Karen took a sip of her wine. Putting the glass down, she followed it up with, 'Until he died, that was. I was widowed two years ago. The farm went bust at around the same time. I've always wanted children and regretted that we didn't have them before his death because now I have nothing that was ours.' Symbolically she spread her empty palms. Her speech was delivered with a

4

philosophical resignation of spirit which was impressive.

Getting up to sort out the vegetables, Charmian thought: every so often Life gets it absolutely right. Karen's attractive, likes the country, liked being married and is a widow. So there's none of the baggage that disillusioned divorcees carry around. She wants children, Giles adores children. It's all in place for Giles. All he has to do is consciously notice her, really *see* her as opposed to just looking at her. *And I think he already has.*

And what will I do? Charmian asked herself, draining sprouts.

Quite apart from heartache, there would be empty weekends. The other lovers were all married and Charmian knew full well that the hallmark of mistresses of married men was that they were generally at a loose end at Christmas, Easter and weekends. Most of all at weekends. Hitherto this had not mattered, but now it would. Turning her attention to the potatoes, she caught herself thinking, I probably can't go on like this. Eventually my looks will start to go and before they do I should perhaps think of settling down. Otherwise I will end up alone. But who would want me, given my odd ideas on independence and the fact that I don't want children?

'Is there a gravy, Giles?' (Knowing that there was not.)

Sounding fugitive Giles said, 'Sort of.'

They both stared at the greasy mess in the bottom of the roasting tin. 'If you don't mind waiting, I'll make one,' offered Charmian. 'Why don't you go and sit down?'

Gratefully he did so. Karen, one elbow on the table, her chin resting on her hand was pensively staring into her wine glass. The quality of her silence was such that nobody felt awkward. As well as everything else she appeared to possess the inestimable gift of repose. Her hair, piled on top of her head apart from several long stray curls which delicately framed her face, gave her a Hardy-esque look. Bathsheba Everdene rather than Tess, though. Not as vulnerable as Tess, decided Charmian, in spite of her bereavement.

Giles said, 'I feel I should apologize for my lack of tact just now, I'm sorry.'

'Nothing to apologize for.' The luminosity of her candlelit smile was unexpected. 'I'm almost over it now. Or rather, I've

5

come to terms with the loss. I loved him and he's gone. That's it.'

Before he stood up to help Charmian, Giles's blond head inclined fractionally towards Karen's, in acknowledgement of what? Her gallantry perhaps. Or her beauty. For Charmian suddenly saw that Karen was beautiful.

At the end of the meal they sat outside. The air had warmed up again, although the closeness was not as oppressive as before. One of Giles's cats materialized from a flowerbed and, having afforded Charmian only the most minimal of greetings, jumped onto Karen's lap.

Now that *does* irritate me, thought Charmian, watching it. Even though I don't like them particularly and it probably senses it, after all the disgusting little bowls I've put down for that animal one would think it could at least afford me the time of day.

Giles went into the house to put a record on his ancient player. Moving like a somnambulist towards inner knowledge, he chose Mozart, and sitting in the wet, sweet-smelling garden the three of them listened to the Trio from *Così fan tutte*, whose haunting singing reverberated in the still summer night air long after the music had come to an end.

In the middle of the following week, Charmian got home late from an evening out with Nigel Guest. Of all her answer phone messages, and there were quite a few including two from current lovers, the one which caught Charmian's attention had been left by her half-sister, Alexandra Curtis.

She checked her watch.

It was getting on for midnight. All the same the uncharacteristically expressionless voice of her sister had said, 'Ring *whatever* time you get back. I have to talk.' A call at that hour of the morning was not likely to be popular with Oliver, her brother-in-law, Charmian recognized. On the other hand, maybe Oliver was not there. Something was plainly wrong and maybe the something was that the Curtises had split up. She entertained this notion only briefly before dismissing it. Although like everybody the Curtises had their rows, on the whole their marriage looked like being durable. She rang the number.

'Alexandra, it's Charmian. Sorry to ring so late. I've only just got back. Is there a problem?'

'Yes, there is,' said Alexandra. 'On Friday Oliver was fired.'

There was a profound silence at the other end of the line. Charmian, who ran her own PR firm and therefore mixed in more various circles than most, had not actually had any dealings with Circumference but nevertheless knew of its Chief Executive, Reg Spivey, by reputation. Oliver had run one of the company's subsidiaries.

Eventually, 'Spivey's a ruthless power freak who's not as clever as he thinks he is,' pronounced the unbiased sister. 'Word has it that the City no longer rates him. Maybe that's why he got rid of Oliver. Too successful and too close for comfort.'

'I don't know.' The catch in Alexandra's voice was audible. 'But whatever the reason, it doesn't help us.' She sounded dazed.

Charmian said, 'How's Oliver holding up?'

'Well, so far, but he's going to be very busy for the next few days sorting out the chaos into which our financial affairs have been thrown. To be honest I don't think the shock has really hit him yet. The worst thing of all will be if he doesn't land another comparable job straight away. You can imagine the prospect of Oliver without enough to occupy him.'

Listening, it was clear to Charmian that after a reversal such as this it would probably take her brother-in-law at least a year to get himself back on his feet. In the case of Dominic Goddard, who had had a similar career accident and with whom she was having dinner next week, it had taken two years, and even then he had never re-established at quite the same level. It looked as though her much-loved sister might be in for a long haul. Charmian stared into the middle distance, conscious of a feeling of outrage and of a vengeful desire not just to help but to settle this particular score. Nothing to be done now, however.

In the end, she said, 'Alexandra, I'm going to have to go to bed, I've got a breakfast meeting tomorrow with an important client. Oliver will need you to himself for the next few days but when things begin to settle down let's meet. By the way, where *is* Oliver?'

'Gleneagles.'

'*Gleneagles*? I didn't know he played golf!'

'He doesn't. Look, I'll tell you all about it when I see you. Let's have a drink together, or come over here for supper if you like.'

'No. As things stand that would be an intrusion into private grief. Oh, and Alexandra . . .' Charmian paused.

'Yes?'

'You're the key to it. You have to hold up. If you don't, he won't.'

'I've worked that out. I'd have gone into the garden for a therapeutic scream but I dare not give way.'

'Poor you. I'll ring you tomorrow. And, remember it isn't the end of the world.'

Monday was Dominic Goddard night and since the only play he and Charmian wanted to see was fully booked, they settled for dinner together. There was a lull as they both scrutinized the menu. Trying to decide between steak tartare and duckling, Charmian said, 'Have you been following the Circumference upheaval?'

'Vaguely,' replied Dominic. 'It had a depressingly familiar ring to me. Odd though, because word has it that Curtis was very effective.'

'I think I might have the foie gras to start with. Have you ever met him?'

Charmian did not disclose her own connection here.

'Yes, I did. Years ago at some function or other. I couldn't claim to know him. He has a stylish wife, I seem to remember. I can't decide between the foie gras and the asparagus.'

'Have the foie gras. It makes the wine easier.'

'Okay, maybe I will. I know the aggressor, Spivey, better than Curtis.'

Well, well. Here was an unexpected piece of good luck. Seek and ye shall find. Charmian did not immediately pick up on this nugget of information, but said instead, 'What about the second course? Steak tartare for me plus a green salad, I think.' She closed the menu.

'You look far too sylphlike to be such a carnivore,' said Dominic. 'Mine's the coq au vin.'

He seized the wine list.

'What were we talking about? Oh, yes, Circumference. It's years since I last met Spivey and he wasn't very nice then. I don't suppose he's improved with age.'

'What sort of a person is he?' Charmian was carefully casual.

Dominic thought for a minute. 'Intimidatingly large, corpulent with it, and very vain, by which I mean he dyes his hair *and* his eyebrows. I suppose I could sum him up by saying he's an unpleasant bully with a predictable penchant for vast camel hair coats to match his vast bulk. You couldn't miss him in a crowd. Must be close to retirement, I should have thought. He's sixty if he's a day.'

'Is there a Mrs Spivey?'

Dominic cast his mind back. 'Yes. Or there used to be. Made no impact on me at all. Why are you so interested anyway?'

Ultra-casual by now, Charmian said, 'I'm not really. It just suddenly occurred to me to wonder what makes that sort of person tick.'

'Oh, in his case that's easy. His parents came over here from Latvia during the war. Ergo I'm willing to bet he'd kill for some sort of quintessential English honour. Lord Spivey of Chipping Ongar or wherever his rose-covered country cottage is, that sort of thing, so that he can feel a social success by throwing his considerable weight about in his local club. And if that ass Hugo Rattray-Smythe has anything to do with it, Spivey'll probably get it too. Reward for services rendered before Reg retires. Can we stop talking about him. It's spoiling my foie gras. Let's talk about us instead.'

Later, as they left the restaurant, Charmian said, 'Your place or mine?'

'Has to be yours tonight; Laura's in town.' Laura was Dominic's wife.

Charmian raised her eyebrows. '*Laura's in town?* Out of interest, where does she think *you* are?'

'At a meeting.' Dominic was sheepish. 'Well, I am, in a manner of speaking.'

'Yes, in a manner of speaking I suppose you are! You should be careful. One day your sins will find you out.'

'Not until I've made love to you, I hope!'

9

Later that night, when Dominic had finally gone, Charmian lay in bed considering what he had told her. I shall have to infiltrate the upper echelons of Circumference, she decided. In order to prevent the thoroughly undeserved elevation of Spivey, I shall have to ensnare Hugo Rattray-Smythe. Assuming Dominic is right, and I'll bet he is, it would be an artistic revenge and very telling. There must be someone among all the contacts I have who can get me an introduction. She briefly entertained the idea of quizzing the gossip columnist Julian Cazalet, who, although not a lover (too indiscreet, which was, after all, the name of his particular game) was close enough for Charmian to ask the occasional favour, but rejected this on the same grounds. Maybe Nigel Guest, advertising, Wednesdays, was the answer. Circumference must have an agency and although she recognized that it would be too much to hope that Nigel's own would be the one, he knew everybody who was anybody in that particular neck of the woods. He could make a connection for her, if he felt like it – and by the time I've finished with him on Wednesday night he will feel like it, predicted Charmian.

TRAVELLING HOPEFULLY
Maggie Makepeace

'A witty and incisive book . . . quirky and sophisticated humour'
CATHOLIC HERALD

For Imogen Redcliffe leaving a man with an incurable disease was unthinkable. But it didn't stop her longing for her freedom.

Perhaps therefore it was dangerous to embark on a holiday with a group of strangers? Two weeks in Seychelles may have seemed like paradise on paper but the reality would prove rather different. In the company of, among others, a sex-starved doctor, a shrewd psychotherapist and a frightened vegetarian, Imogen is forced to face up to her own shortcomings and to take action.

It's a liberating experience but not quite in the way she intended!

Praise for Maggie Makepeace's *Breaking the Chain*

'Sparkling comedy and high-value entertainment' SUNDAY TIMES

FACING THE MUSIC
Mary Sheepshanks

'There wouldn't be any trouble if only you had a wife,' Lady Boynton had said. But Flavia Cameron was not at all what she had in mind for Gervaise Henderson. Impossibly young, with a musical talent that could have been heard in concert halls around the world, the headmaster's new wife was beautiful and sparkling and she swept the Upper Fourth off their feet.

Until Ben Forbes arrived, with a father who saw Flavia not as a prodigy, a daughter or a wife, but, for the first time, as herself. It is a discovery that will throw her life into turmoil.

Perceptive and poignant, funny and touching, *Facing the Music* is a welcome new novel from the author of *A Price for Everything*.

Praise for *A Price for Everything*:

'Touchingly wise and extremely funny' THE TIMES

'Midway between the sexual candour of Mary Wesley and Joanna Trollope's sharp observation' MAIL ON SUNDAY

Available from July 4th

PARTY PIECES
Amanda MacAndrew

Charlotte Forth had been twenty-one, newly out of work, and impressionable. Small wonder that she fell prey to Robin Brand, Oxford graduate and aspiring politician, in search of a rich wife with fine ankles.

It may not be easy, she thinks charitably, to have a rich wife, but it isn't a doddle being one either. Over-valued (for her fortunes are locked away in trust for their twins) and under-appreciated, Charlotte does her best to resist two addictions: a political journalist of overwhelming compatibility and a secret which becomes more public by the day.

By the time Robin has secured himself a safe seat through his astute nose for a by-election, his soothing speeches and magnetic performances are put to parliamentary use only. So when Charlotte is door-stepped by a journalist one fine autumn day in 1994, asking whether she will stand by her husband in the light of his resignation as Minister for Youth, will the amenable, compliant, perfect parliamentary wife toe the Party line?

Available from August 1st

THE ANNIVERSARY
Ann Swinfen

The most evocative and compelling family novel since Rosamunde Pilcher's *The Shellseekers*, *The Anniversary* sweeps the reader into the fabric of a family, a community and an era.

It is June 11th 1994 in the depths of Herefordshire and Natasha Devereux's family and two hundred guests gather together to celebrate the fiftieth anniversary of St. Martins. From the vision of one woman who fled Bolshevik Russia and opened her doors to artists, musicians, writers and refugees from war-torn Europe it has become a sanctuary for five generations of a family who – over the course of one day – face marital crisis, impending birth, teenage trauma, a father's roving eye into forbidden territory, momentous news from the past, communal financial crisis, and a lost love from the summer of '57.

As the evening shadows spread-eagle across the lawn to the rambling house and the great old copper beech, Natasha comes to the fruition of her life's work. The kaleidoscope of memory has been shaken, decisions have been taken. There has been a birth, and a death, but above all a celebration.

£1 OFF

A special offer to you when you buy
Elizabeth Palmer's
Flowering Judas

Just complete this voucher and take it into any participating bookshop and receive £1 off the cover price.

Name

Address

_____

Postcode

Name of Bookshop/town

Authorisation by bookshop staff

_____

(Dear bookseller: just sign here and return this voucher to:
Dept WF, Arrow Marketing Dept, Random House,
20 Vauxhall Bridge Road, London SW1V 2SA
or the supplying wholesaler)

Offer only valid in UK & Eire.
Offer closes on December 25th 1996.

ISBN 0-09-916642-9

From time to time Arrow would like
to send you more information about
similar books that might interest you.

☐ Please tick here if you do not
   want to receive any more
   information from us.

9 780099 166429